LETHAL LADY

Duke yelled, "I'm going after the woman!"

"No," Lester roared. "Get Fargo first, then we'll get her!"

"Like hell you will!" Melody shouted.

Fargo saw Duke's head peek around a large cottonwood to sight a six-gun. It was enough of a target. He blew a hunk of Duke away. "You're next, Lester," he said.

"No, Mr. Fargo!" Melody cried. "Let me get the son of a bitch."

Her rifle fired. Lester spun halfway around from the force of the bullet going through him.

Fargo caught Melody's look of triumph as she finished off Lester. He sure hated to admit it, but the little lady was one helluva killer!

THE
TRAILSMAN
101

SHOSHONI
SPIRITS

by

Jon Sharpe

A SIGNET BOOK

SIGNET
Published by the Penguin Group
Penguin Books USA Inc., 375 Hudson Street, New York,
New York 10014, U.S.A.
Penguin Books Ltd, 27 Wrights Lane, London W8 5TZ, England
Penguin Books Australia Ltd, Ringwood, Victoria, Australia
Penguin Books Canada Ltd, 2801 John Street, Markham,
Ontario, Canada L3R 1B4
Penguin Books (N.Z.) Ltd, 182-190 Wairau Road, Auckland 10, New Zealand

Penguin Books Ltd, Registered Offices: Harmondsworth, Middlesex, England

First published by Signet, an imprint of Penguin Books USA Inc.

First Printing, May, 1990
10 9 8 7 6 5 4 3 2 1

The first chapter of this book previously appeared in *Riverboat Gold,* the
one-hundredth volume in this series.

 REGISTERED TRADEMARK—MARCA REGISTRADA

Printed in the United States of America

PUBLISHER'S NOTE
This is a work of fiction. Names, characters, places, and incidents either are
the product of the author's imagination or are used fictitiously, and any
resemblance to actual persons, living or dead, events, or locales is entirely
coincidental.

BOOKS ARE AVAILABLE AT QUANTITY DISCOUNTS WHEN USED TO PROMOTE PRODUCTS
OR SERVICES. FOR INFORMATION PLEASE WRITE TO PREMIUM MARKETING DIVISION,
PENGUIN BOOKS USA INC., 375 HUDSON STREET, NEW YORK, NEW YORK 10014.

Wyoming, 1860, the Rocky Mountain high country, where conniving women and dangerous men tested the ancient Shoshoni spirits, who passed down a terrible judgment in a cannon's roar . . .

1

The Ovaro's ears perked and swiveled. Trusting his horse's keen hearing, the big man reined to a halt and turned to look behind him. Faint sounds spilled over the flat top of the long rise. After a few studious seconds, he spurred the pinto up the grassy slope until he could see over the crest.

Less than a mile down the rutted trail, a cloud of Nebraska dust boiled behind the unmistakable shape of a stagecoach coming hard and fast. The bark of rifles meant only one thing: Cheyenne, as many as twenty.

The big man rode back down to the base of the rise where he spurred the stallion to a gallop. Within minutes, he had closed the distance and charged up the slope to come abreast of the stage.

The man riding shotgun knelt amid luggage on the roof, firing off shots at the pony-mounted braves racing forward in the billowing dust. Passengers fired from the windows.

Skye Fargo added his Colt's firepower to that from the coach. Two half-naked Cheyenne toppled to the ground as Fargo's bullets tore into them. He reloaded while moving in closer.

An arrow streaked out of the dust. The man on the stage roof screamed and clutched his shoulder. He rolled out of the luggage, but stopped short of falling off the roof.

Fargo emptied the Colt into the band of Cheyenne, holstered the weapon, and drew his Sharps from its saddle case.

Before he could fire, three Cheyenne broke from the pack and headed toward him. The war-painted riders brandished long war clubs. Fargo shot the nearest savage off his pony, then reined the Ovaro between the other two. As he charged through the tight gap, he slammed the Sharp's barrel against one warrior's head, then caught the other on the chest with the backswing. Glancing over his shoulder, he watched both men roll on the sunbaked ground.

He turned the pinto to avoid the dust and headed for the stage. During the movement, his keen wild-creature hearing discerned a new sound over that made by the rumbling stagecoach and gunfire. He swerved out and glanced behind the cloud. Three horsemen chased in, firing point-blank at the unsuspecting Cheyenne. He waved for them to move right to get out of the passenger's line of fire. As a unit the three riders veered right.

Fargo reloaded the Colt while he dropped back to protect the left side of the stagecoach. With the other defenders, Fargo fired blindly into the dense swirling cloud. Four warriors tumbled on the ground.

Contained on three sides, the Cheyenne wisely broke off their assault. They headed toward hills and ravines to the north.

The trio of gunmen at the right rear turned to give pursuit. Fargo angled northwest to block for them. Before the Cheyenne made it to safety in gulches, three more were shot off their mounts. Fargo and the others halted.

Returning to the stage, which had stopped down the trail, the men joined Fargo. Two were rawboned youngsters, not yet twenty. Both clean-shaven young men had steel-blue eyes. Tufts of flaxen hair poked out from under the sweatbands of their wide-brimmed hats. While they weren't identical twins, Fargo guessed they might be related.

The third had a leathery face with a scar across his nose. His unruly hair, beard, and mustache were rust-colored, his sunken eyes dark-green. Fargo fixed his age at thirty-five. He doubted the man was kin to the others.

All wore brown leather gun belts low on their hips, the bottoms of the holsters held close to their thighs with leather thongs. Each carried a single-action, five-shot Joslyn Army revolver. The youngsters, he noted, wore their guns on the left.

One of the younger men grinned as he said, "Mister, you got guts bigger'n St. Louis. I saw you takin' them Cheyenne with that rifle. Hell, we rode on in just so we could watch you whip 'em."

Fargo chuckled. "You men couldn't have come along at a better time." He offered his hand. "My name's Skye Fargo."

"Glad to meetcha. Mine's Richard Dotson. Most call me Rick." He nodded toward the other young rider. "He's Calvin Boggs, my cousin. Cal, he don't talk much as me, but he's damn fast with a gun. Ain't that right, Cal?"

Calvin gave no indication he heard Rick brag about him. Rick looked at the older man. "That's one of our uncles, Leon McAdoo. Leon, he don't say much, either. That's 'cause some of his tongue got cut off. Where you headed, Mr. Fargo?"

"West. Yourself?"

Rick pulled on an earlobe. "Nowhere in particular. Might say we're looking around."

Fargo knew better than that. Men didn't wander just for the hell of it. They either had a destination in mind or were running, usually from the law. Whichever, it was their business. He didn't probe, although their appearance behind the stage in open country, coupled with their handiness with the Joslyns, was a mite suspicious.

At the stagecoach, Fargo was mildly surprised to see three women among the men huddled around the wounded man. They'd stretched him out on his back in a patch of shade.

One of the women, a shapely strawberry blonde, stood next to a fleshy, young brunette. A tall, willowy ash-blond woman a few years younger than Fargo looked over the brunette's shoulder.

Fargo dismounted. The injured man's eyes were closed, his breathing shallow. The arrow was embedded deep in the flesh above and slightly left of his left breast. To pull the arrow out was unthinkable; the added damage could easily kill the man. Fargo squatted to break off the feathered fletch.

The strawberry blonde gasped, "Sir, what are you doing?"

Fargo didn't answer right away. He lifted the man's upper torso so he could shove the arrow on through the shoulder. The unconscious man groaned. Pulling it out by the flint arrowhead, Fargo said, "Saving his life. I need a bandage." He looked up at the woman. "Don't just stand there. One of you rip off a long piece of petticoat hem."

In unison they stiffened and raised their hands to their bosoms.

Fargo selected the ash blonde. "You are wearing a petticoat, aren't you?"

"Uh, er, of course," she stammered. She glanced about the faces fixed on her.

Fargo handed her his throwing knife. "Step into the stage and cut off a strip."

While she followed his orders, Fargo addressed the sweat-soaked stage driver, a short, beefy older man. "Fort Hope's what—about an hour away?"

"More or less," the fellow grunted. "Probably more. Is Charley gonna make it?"

"He might, if you put another lather on your team. Soon as I get him bandaged to stop the bleeding, I'll ride shotgun for you."

The brunette's eyes flared. She asked, "Shotgun? Are you saying they might come back?"

"Wouldn't know," Fargo replied. "Might, might not."

The stage door opened. The ash blonde descended, then handed a length of white material and the knife to Fargo. He tore off two pieces for compresses and used the rest to bind them in place. The two male passengers helped him lay the wounded man on the forward seat.

Fargo said, "Okay, ladies, you can get aboard now." He glanced at the two male passengers. Fargo told them to sit on the floor and hold the wounded man on the seat.

After tying the Ovaro behind the stagecoach, Fargo climbed up next to the driver. The grizzly old man snapped the reins on the horse's backs. The coach lurched forward, Dotson and his kin following.

A dusty hour later, they saw Fort Hope, which stood on the bank of the North Fork of the Platte River. Settlers, not the military, had built the small town in the Nebraska panhandle near Wyoming Territory. Muffled sounds of gunfire greeted the stage.

Fargo motioned for Rick to come alongside. Rick moved in and looked up at him. Fargo yelled, "How about bringing my horse to me?"

Rick nodded and fell back.

The driver asked, "What're you up to, mister?"

"I'll ride ahead to see what all the commotion's about and fetch a doc for Charley."

"Hell, mister, this is Fort Hope. That shooting don't mean nothing. Happens all the time. Letting off steam."

"Yeah, well, I'll go check it out, anyhow."

Rick brought the Ovaro alongside. Fargo stepped down into the saddle. He dropped back to warn the women, "Be ready to duck, ladies. We're coming into town. I hear some gunfire, so I'm going ahead to make sure it's safe." He touched the brim of his hat and galloped ahead.

Fargo entered the little frontier town on its main street. All movement had ceased. The few people he saw were crouched behind something solid, protective. The ruckus came from the crossroads near the far end of Fort Hope. Riding toward it, Fargo saw two men sprawled facedown in the dust, and a chubby woman who sat with her back against a water trough. She was screaming and clutching her bloody left thigh. He rode by the two men, who lay in pools of muddy blood.

Closer to the crossroad, he saw, an armed man stood guard outside the door of the little bank. Seven horses were ground-reined in front of him. Without warning, the man fired at Fargo.

The Trailsman dug his heels into the stallion's flanks and charged in, firing the Colt. The bullet's impact catapulted the man through the bank window.

Fargo slid from the saddle and ran to plaster his back against the outside wall of the bank. He yelled, "Throw your guns out. Follow them and you won't get hurt."

He listened to boots scuffle on the wooden floor inside the bank, then an exchange of whispers. A moment passed before a lone six-gun arched out through the doorway. A bearded man wearing a torn duster stepped outside.

Twin black eyes filled with meanness stared at Fargo. As the robber fell left, his hand darted inside the duster. Fargo squeezed the trigger. A nasty red hole appeared in the man's forehead. "Okay," he began, "I know there's five more of you in there. I'm giving you three seconds to come out. You can come shooting or with your hands empty. Makes no difference to me. One . . . two . . ."

A man hurtled through the shattered window and tumbled toward the horses. Fargo shot him in the thigh. The man yelped and struggled to crawl between two horses. A second shot stopped him before he succeeded.

A high-pitched female voice inside the bank yelled, "Out back! They're getting away out back."

Fargo pushed away from the wall, and dashed around the corner of the building. One of the robbers leapt from behind the bank. His left hand gripped a canvas bag, his right a six-gun. Fargo's single shot caught the man in the face.

He peered around the corner of the bank. The other three men were already on saddled horses at the rear of a feed store. As they fled, Fargo stepped out and emptied his Colt at them, but missed. He reloaded as he went to retrieve the bag.

As he entered the bank a woman's head popped up behind a teller's cage. Her terrified eyes stared at the big Colt. "Don't shoot me," she begged. "I got kids at home."

He holstered the Colt. "You can get up now. It's safe." He pitched the bag on the counter. "You all alone?"

"No." Her eyes darted to the door of the walk-in safe. "Mr. Theodore—"

Fargo vaulted over the counter. He swung the door open. A man staggered out. "You Theodore?" Fargo asked.

The man groaned, "Yes. Take what you want, but don't hurt us."

"I'm not a robber. Those who aren't dead are hightailing it out of town."

The dazed banker's senses returned instantly. He smiled, stuck his hand out, and said, "This has been a bad day."

Fargo could believe that. He shook the banker's hand. Through an easy grin he said, "Yeah, well, nobody said banking on the frontier would be easy. You all right? I need to be going."

"Yes. Thank you for what you did. Let me reward you." He reached for several stacks of bills on a shelf.

"No reward necessary, Mr. Theodore. Thanks just the same." Fargo crawled over the counter and went outside.

A crowd had gathered in the intersection. To no one in particular he asked where he'd find the livery. Nearly everybody pointed up the main street. Fargo whistled for the pinto. It trotted up to him. He eased into the saddle, tipped his hat to the crowd, and headed up the street.

After stabling and looking after his horse, he carried his saddlebags and Sharps to the small hotel. The stagecoach waited out front. Before entering, Fargo paused to inquire whether the wounded man had survived the final leg of the trip.

"Yeah, thanks to you, Charley's gonna be okay,"

the crusty old man replied. "He's at the doc's house. You're a helluva man, mister. First you come out of nowhere to help beat off redskins hunting scalps, then take care of a dying man, then damned if you don't shoot it out with bank robbers and leave four of 'em dead in the dirt. Mister, I'd ride straight into hell with you."

Fargo chuckled. As he turned to go through the doorway, he bumped into pillowy softness. The brunette gasped and embraced him to keep her balance. He grabbed her around the shoulders. Their eyes met. Her hug tightened. He felt her nipples punch into him.

"Excuse me, ma'am," he apologized. "That was clumsy of me."

She stood back, smiling up at him. "No harm done, big man. See you around."

Fargo noticed she added some swing to her hips as she walked across the street to the saloon. He stepped to the desk and paid for a room.

The cheery female clerk handed him the key. "Ground floor, third door on the right. Let me know if you want anything—extra pillow, additional warmth . . . anything. We strive to please."

Fargo nodded and went to his room. The large bed was firm. He liked that. The one window was closed and locked, but had no curtain. He didn't like that. He stood the Sharps against the wall next to the headboard, put the saddlebags on the bureau, and left to go to the saloon.

He paused at the double doors to look inside. Standing with others at the long bar were the stagecoach driver, his two male passengers, and the threesome who helped fend off the Cheyenne. Four smiling saloon girls were obviously offering their services to the new arrivals.

He recognized the barrel-chested bartender, busy pouring drinks. Nearly everybody had considered Earl Pulmar a permanent fixture in Miss Lillian's elegant saloon in Silver Junction, Colorado. Fargo wondered what in hell prompted the man to leave her for this dump.

The three women from the stage occupied a poker table immediately behind the men at the bar. The two taller, older females had beers before them. The soft brunette he had bumped into sipped whiskey from a shot glass. Their presence clearly annoyed the buxom whores who watched them out the corners of their eyes.

Fargo pushed through the swinging doors. He wedged between the cousins halfway down the bar.

Earl glanced up and beamed, "Well, I'll be god-damned . . . Skye Fargo. What're you doing in Fort Hope?" He shoved a ham of a hand across the bar to Fargo.

Fargo shook it. "Thought I'd ask you the same thing. Good to see you again, Earl. I'm passing through on my way to Washington. How's Miss Lillian?"

Earl's normal joviality gave way to sadness. After a long pause, he sighed, "She's dead, Fargo."

Fargo grimaced. "I'm sorry to hear that. What happened?"

"One night after the saloon closed, somebody—a man, for sure—shot her, but only after she put up one hell of a fight. Her room was a mess. All her jewelry and money were gone. We think a drifter did it."

Fargo shook his head slowly. "And the drifter?"

"Got away. But not before she bit off a hunk of his tongue. We found it in her mouth."

Stiffening, Fargo drew his Colt. He stepped back.

Leon McAdoo was nowhere in sight. . . .

2

The room quieted. Fargo looked at the cousins for an answer. Rick made it a point to keep his gunhand clear of the Joslyn's handle. He met Fargo's hard stare and spoke in a no-nonsense tone. "Cal and me, we don't know nothing about what you and this feller were saying. Leon told us two men held him down while another whacked it off. We don't want no trouble with you, mister. That's the truth."

Before Fargo could respond, the willowy blonde spoke up. "Leave them alone, mister. They helped save us from those savages. Remember?"

Fargo glanced at her, then back at Rick. Holstering the Colt, he said, "A wrong and a right doesn't make a right. When you see your uncle, tell him if I ever learn he set foot in Silver Junction, I'll come looking for him. When I find him, I'll kill him on the spot, no questions asked. Do you understand?"

Rick smirked. "Yeah, we understand. But you're not scaring us, mister." He turned to Earl and ordered another drink.

Fargo moved down the bar. The cousins watched him in the long mirror behind the bar. Conversations picked up, breaking the tension.

The strawberry-blond passenger pushed back from the poker table and came to stand behind Fargo. After clearing her throat to gain his attention, she spoke in a voice loud enough for most to hear. "Sir, I want to thank you for what you did earlier on the trail. I owe my life to you and the other men who risked their own to protect me . . . all of us."

Fargo rested the small of his back on the edge of the bar and considered the woman. She stood about five-six, had broad shoulders, and a wasp waist. He guessed she might be twenty-five, her weight not more than 115 pounds. The dark-green irises looking at him were clear, the big eyes framed by long eyelashes that curled nicely. From the way she carried herself, he figured she was a proper lady, one with proper education from a school back East. Decent women didn't frequent saloons. And this one wore a wedding ring.

He said, "No thanks necessary, ma'am. That was all in a day's work out here on the frontier. Where might you and the others be headed? I notice you're married but don't have a man at your side."

"You're very observant." She glanced at the bartender, then back at him. "Did I hear correctly? Your name is Skye Fargo?"

Fargo nodded.

Earl amplified. "Ma'am, they call him the Trailsman. That's because Fargo knows the West better than anyone. He's been all over at least twice."

She looked at Fargo anew. He watched a thought form in her eyes. She addressed his question about her marital status. "I wear the ring although I'm a widow. My husband, Lieutenant Julian Abbott, was murdered by Indians this past summer."

Every eye in the room cut onto her.

"Sorry to hear that," Fargo replied, "but I'm sure he knew most Indians and cavalry don't mix too well. You didn't say where you're headed." When she arched an eyebrow, he added, "While it's none of my business, a lady like you doesn't seem to fit in way out here."

"You are correct, Mr. Fargo. I do not belong on the frontier. Actually, I abhor the frontier, the daily misery it causes, and the uncertainty. However, I must suffer it one more time. I'm going to Seattle to make a new life for myself. I plan to establish a clothing shop for fine ladies."

He nodded, and she continued. "I'm not one to

eavesdrop, but I couldn't keep from overhearing you mention your destination is also Washington Territory. Is that correct?"

"Yes, ma'am. I leave at sunrise tomorrow."

"I need assistance, sir. I'll pay you handsomely to escort me. Will five hundred dollars be satisfactory?"

He answered, "More than." She made it sound like a foregone conclusion he would take her with him. The pretty woman had gall, and he liked that. He let his gaze move down and up her slowly to emphasize his next comment and make sure she had no reservations about it. "It's a long journey, one that will be hard and tiring, not to mention dangerous. We'll pass through hostile Indian country. I don't think I have to tell an army wife about the possible dangers there. Finally, once we start, there's no turning back, meaning if you weaken I'll—"

Her upraised hand stopped him. "Mr. Fargo, don't let my size or femininity deceive you into thinking I'm some kind of a delicate flower that wilts outside of a parlor. I'm accustomed to hardship. I won't weaken or slow you down in any way. My family raises Thoroughbreds in Kentucky. I can outride most men. And I am an expert with rifle and revolver. As for the Indians, I'll take my chances. Again, I won't be a burden to you. Will you take me?"

"Yes. Be at the livery by sunup. By the way, Mrs. Abbott, what's your first name?"

"Melody." She grinned. "Sounds down right sweet and harmless, wouldn't you agree?"

Fargo recognized a hellcat when he saw and heard one. Nodding, he shared her grin. He touched the brim of his hat to seal the bargain.

Melody Abbott turned and walked from the saloon. As she stepped off the porch, the ash blonde rose and left.

Earl said, "Fargo, you might have put your foot in the bucket this time. Better watch that filly. There's something about her that tells me she's got a wicked streak."

Fargo swiveled around and handed him the empty glass. "One more, Earl, then tell me where I'll find food. I can handle her. Army wives are accustomed to taking orders."

Earl answered while filling the glass with whiskey. "Yeah, you hope. There's something you need to know, but now isn't the time. Why don't you drop by later, after the crowd thins out? The café's around the corner. Follow your nose. Tell Pokraka I sent you." Earl moved down the bar.

Fargo stared at his own reflection in the mirror, wondering if he'd been suckered by the pert widow. Tossing down the drink, he told himself he'd know soon enough. He put a silver dollar on the bar for Earl and left for the café.

A behemoth of a man wearing a white apron stood behind the café's counter. He was watching the tall ash blond who sat alone at a table, picking at the platter of roast beef before her.

Fargo settled down on a stool at the counter and told the man Earl had sent him.

Pokraka cracked a wide smile. "Earl's my pal. We got roast today. Want it or breakfast?"

"Take the roast," the blonde suggested.

Fargo swung around to face her, but spoke to Pokraka. "I'll go with the lady's recommendation."

She favored him with a winsome smile that suggested more than a passing amenity. "I don't bite. Why don't you join me? We'll chat while we eat."

Fargo moved and sat across from her. "You have me at the disadvantage, ma'am. Your name is . . ."

"Victoria. Victoria Ellison. So you won't wonder, I'm thirty-two, single, and grateful. I suppose you know she'll end up getting you killed."

Pokraka arrived with Fargo's meal. During the pause, Fargo decided the brassy woman wanted to say more about the widow. He opened the door with questions. "She who? Grateful for what?"

"For saving me from those Indians. You know who—coy little Melody."

"Are you and Mrs. Abbott close friends?"

"Never saw her until we boarded the stage the other day at Fort Kearny. I think she told you only part of the story a while ago. You puzzle me, Fargo."

"Puzzle you? You need to explain that." He poked a piece of roast in his mouth.

She absentmindedly pointed her fork at him for emphasis each time she said "you." "Certainly. You are either naïve, or you are dense, or you simply don't care. I mean, my God, traipsing all over Indian lands with . . ."

He chased the bite of roast with a slug of coffee before replying, "You forgot to mention the money."

Victoria visibly tensed when he said money. Her heretofore relaxed expression became serious, bordering, he thought, on panic. Her hazel eyes widened questioningly as she leaned forward and whispered, "You, you know about the money?"

He wondered how she could have missed hearing Melody Abbott make the monetary offer. "Of course," he answered offhandedly.

Victoria gasped, "How?"

"She told me."

The blonde drew back and stared at him for a moment. Finally, she said, "Oh, you meant the five hundred."

She made it a flat statement, not a question.

Fargo ate more roast and displayed no other reaction. It was apparent Victoria Ellison knew more, much more, about Melody Abbott and her finances, and just as obvious she had no intent to discuss the matter any further. The two women were closer than they appeared. Much closer.

He changed the subject. "Are you heading farther west as well?"

"No, I think I'll winter here in Fort Hope, maybe drift on up to Fort Laramie."

He nodded. "So how do you make your way? I don't figure you one to end up flat on your back except by choice."

She gave him a wry smile. "You got that right. I do okay playing cards."

Fargo downed the remainder of his coffee and pushed back from the table. "It's been nice chatting with you, Victoria. Don't be tempted to draw to inside straights." He paid Pokraka for the meal and left.

Riding into town, he'd seen a sign on the barbershop that offered nickel baths. Fargo walked to the shop and plunked down a nickel. The barber handed him a towel and wash rag and nodded toward the back entrance. "There's a big kettle of boiling water. Help yourself. Soap's on the benches."

A high board fence surrounded the bath area. Four wooden tubs were arranged around the kettle of hot water. The two men from the stage occupied two. Fargo acknowledged the men with nods, then started filling a tub with more hot water than cold.

Both men were huskily built, about the same height, six-footers, and appeared close to their mid-twenties. The tenor voice belonged to Sid and the baritone to Everett. Fargo gathered they'd known each other a long time.

Undressing, he listened to them talk about nothing in particular. He wondered if he'd interrupted a serious conversation. The cost of whiskey in Cincinnati fell in the former category, as did the condition of the soil in Fort Hope, and the mating habits of house sparrows. He forced himself to quit listening, settled down to soak in the hot water, and closed his eyes.

After a few minutes the rhythm and tenor of their talk changed and opened his ears. Sid was asking Everett, "Where'd you go after getting out of the hospital?" Everett didn't answer immediately. Sid probed, "And what did you do?"

Everett answered the last question obliquely. "I damn sure didn't go home. I went to Columbus. Yourself?"

Sid answered readily. "I limped around Denver for a while, then drifted up to Cincinnati to visit a former girlfriend. Shirley threw me out. Claimed my spark had died."

They laughed at the confession, then Everett probed, "So what'er your plans? Out here, I mean. Risky, isn't it?"

"Damn right it is," Sid retorted. "Fort Hope's just a jumping-off point for me. I'm joining the first wagon train heading for Oregon or California. I'm tired of city life, fed up with the plains. I'd die before I'd go back to the farm. You?"

"Not sure, Sid. Denver sounds interesting. I might drop down there and look around. Maybe try my hand at panning for gold. Hell, I don't know."

"Is the belly healed enough for that? You got shot up pretty bad. Should have died. Frankly, I was surprised to see you in Fort Kearny."

"Yeah, I'm healed, good as new. Speaking of surprises, I was amazed to see you on your feet. I reckoned they would have to cut off your legs to save you. How many bullets did that rusty-haired son of a bitch leave in you, anyhow?"

"Eleven altogether. Five from him and the others from his henchmen. The six slugs the doctor found are in a bag in my left pocket. Ballast. I'm okay. The limp's gone. Listen, I have to see a man about a horse."

Fargo heard Sid leave the tub. After he dried down and dressed, he told Everett he'd see him later in the saloon. Fargo heard the rear barbershop door squeak open and close. Within seconds Everett left his tub, wiped his body with the towel, got dressed, and departed.

Fargo assessed what he'd heard. Both men were either gunfighters, ex-lawmen, or ex-army. Whichever, they had ridden together, then parted while in hospitals. Also, they had lied about their destinations. Both tried too hard to make their stories sound convincing. It wasn't what they said, but how they said it. Neither had recovered from their wounds to the point where they'd be comfortable astride a horse, otherwise they wouldn't have taken the stagecoach. Stagecoach? Hhmmmnnn, Fargo mused, five people, all in the same stage after assembling in Fort Kearny, all stopping in Fort Hope to figure out what to do next. Coincidence? Maybe? Earl had said he wanted to talk.

Fargo scrubbed his body clean, pulled on his clothes, and headed for the saloon. Customers packed the place. True to her word, Victoria sat with five men at a poker table. One of the men was the banker, Theodore. They were playing five-card draw. Fargo bellied up to the end of the bar nearest the double doors and waited for Earl to notice him.

Earl slid a bottle of bourbon halfway down the bar to him. Fargo pulled the cork and started drinking. Shortly, Earl came and told him most of the customers were regulars, having a drink before heading home for supper. "When they start leaving, I'll have one of the girls take over back here, and we'll talk." Earl's gaze focused on Victoria. He asked, "You know anything about that woman?"

"No, not really. Why?"

"I swear I've seen her before. Want to say in Denver. If she's the one, she bright-eyed for a man big and tough as you. If she's the same one, she also totes a gun and knows how to use it. Know what I mean?"

Fargo nodded. "That's interesting. Think I'll go spectate. Come get me when you're free." He pushed away from the bar and took the bottle with him. He stood behind and slightly left of Victoria.

She didn't notice him. Neither did the banker, who occupied the seat across from her. Theodore's eyes never looked up from the table. He had his money separated by denominations, with the stack of twenty-dollar gold pieces the largest.

Victoria's poke was lean. Fargo felt sure there was more in the big purse on the floor next to her chair, a hand's dip away, like the grip of the Smith & Wesson he saw in the purse.

A fat man, obviously a merchant from the way he dressed, sat on her left. A cigar stub jutted from one corner of his lips. At least a hundred dollars lay before him. Fargo reckoned that was only the tip of his stash.

He would have more, plenty more, tucked in his inside coat pocket.

On Victoria's right sat a wiry cowpuncher who looked as though he just walked in out of a dust storm. The lack of money in front of him predicted he would soon go back to eating Nebraska dust.

Next to Theodore sat a cheroot-smoking gentleman who showed all the trappings of a riverboat gambler: flat, wide-brimmed black hat, tidy black vest and thigh-length matching coat, red string tie, clean-shaven, two large diamond rings—impeccable. He kept his free hand palm-down on the table to assure everyone he wasn't cheating, and held cards in the right. It appeared he was the big winner so far.

A gangly older man with bushy, unruly silver hair and eyebrows sat on Theodore's right. He was the nervous type, tense, and kept his dark eyes cutting from one player's cards to the next, as though counting them. He too kept his long bony free hand palm-down next to his money on the table. It looked to Fargo as though he was giving the others a run for their money. He won the current hand and the shuffle-up with three deuces.

Fargo watched four hands play out. Victoria won the first with two pair, Theodore the second with a heart flush, the gambling man claimed the third with a full house, nines over queens, and the old man raked in the fourth after dusting off the cowpuncher with a pair of fours. The cowboy's face was beet-red when he stood and spread a ten-high nothing. He cursed all the way to the bar.

"Not my night," the fat man claimed. He moved to the bar, where started serious drinking while fondling a fleshy saloon girl's rump.

The silver-haired man shuffled the deck and dealt. Fargo watched Victoria squeeze out a pair of tens. She opened with a twenty.

Riverboat and Theodore called. Silver Hair raised twenty. Victoria, Theodore, and Gambler each shoved twenty more dollars out into the pot.

Theodore took one card. Victoria took three, and so did Gambler and Silver Hair, who dragged in the discards, then dealt to the others and himself.

Victoria caught a third ten. She bet forty dollars.

Gambler covered and raised fifty.

Theodore called and raised him fifty.

Silver Hair tossed out a hundred and forty, then raised by a hundred.

Fargo watched Victoria start to fold, then change her mind, and call.

Gambler called. After a studious, sweating moment, the banker called and raised a hundred.

Silver Hair didn't hesitate to cover and up it by another hundred.

Victoria calmly covered and raised him a hundred.

Gambler folded.

Theodore shook his head and folded reluctantly.

Silver Hair called her.

Victoria spread her three tens on the table.

Silver Hair spread four sixes. He reached to pull in the pot.

Victoria leveled the Smith & Wesson at him and whispered, "Mister, I think you accidentally got in those discards. Don't move your hands."

Silver Hair sputtered, "Lady, you're crazy. I won fair and square." He glanced up at the faces of those watching and appealed, "You saw everything. Tell her she's mistaken."

Fargo withdrew his Arkansas toothpick, then stepped between Victoria and Silver Hair. Fargo stabbed for the back of the man's hand. Silver Hair jerked his hand away quickly. A red queen fell onto the table.

Victoria squeezed the trigger and blew a hole in the cheating man's forehead.

Fargo jerked the throwing knife away and touched its tip to the back of Gambler's palm-down hand. Gambler swallowed hard. Fargo said, "Mister, you forgot to clean up when you had the chance. Now lift that hand real slow and easy like."

The hand raised. Under it was a card, facedown.

Fargo flipped over the seven of diamonds with the tip of the knife.

The banker rose, his dark eyes blazing, fixed on the card, and drew his gun. Gambler fell backward, scrambled to his feet, and bolted for the back door. Theodore shot him in the back of the head.

Victoria said, "All right, gentlemen, time to make everything right. Let's clean out those buzzards' pockets and split the money." Glancing toward the bar, she offered, "Cowboy, you and fatty want in on this split?"

Within minutes the cheaters' money was divided. Everyone except Theodore left. He and Fargo moved to the bar for drinks. Earl nodded toward a table and led the way. He handed Fargo a fresh bottle of bourbon and set three glasses on the table. "Be with you after I drag the dead out back," he said.

Theodore asked, "How did they do it? Why didn't I see it? Looks like they would've cheated with aces, not those cards. I don't get it."

Fargo explained, "The value of the palmed card makes no difference. Sooner or later it will make a hand. The old man palmed a six several hands back. He caught a pair of sixes on that last deal. Then, damned if he didn't find the fourth six on the draw. In case you didn't notice, both he and the gambler you shot used both hands to pick up their cards. When the old man saw those sixes, he inserted the one he had palmed and replaced it with the queen. Eventually, he'd have need for the queen.

"Same with the slick gambler. He swapped the seven for the jack he had palmed. Victoria saw them do it. All she did was wait until she had a big pot before exposing them. Don't feel bad. It takes a bright-eyed player like Victoria to catch card cheaters."

They made small talk while Earl towed the old man outside by the ankles. He came back dusting his hands and said, "I was wrong about seeing her in Denver. It was in Miss Lillian's place. A man with dark-red hair was with her. Fargo, the kid you called Rick?"

"Yeah, what about him?"

"One of the men he came in with; has an ugly scar across his nose?"

"His uncle, Leon McAdoo. And?"

"I didn't recognize him. That's because he didn't have that scar when he came to Silver Junction. Fargo, I'd swear he murdered Miss Lillian. He hung around in the saloon for two days. She caught him snooping in her office and had me throw him out in the street. I warned him to get out of town and never come back. He said he'd get even. Another thing. That woman you're taking west, Melody Abbott? She didn't tell you everything."

"Not by a long shot," Theodore added quickly.

"Oh?" Fargo mused.

Theodore delivered a digested version of what happened. "Four months ago, early July, an army payroll wagon was ambushed on the road between here and Fort Laramie. According to eyewitnesses, a white man backed up by about twenty Indians armed with carbines was responsible for the near massacre, and theft. They made off with the entire payroll, one hundred thousand dollars. The little lady's husband was the officer in charge of the payroll detachment.

"The witnesses, two badly wounded troopers, said Lieutenant Abbott was also shot up and left for dead. After it was all over and the attackers had left, they say Abbott climbed on his horse and rode after them. Abbott hasn't been seen or heard from since then. The army conducted a thorough search and didn't find his body or his horse."

Earl expanded on Theodore's accounting. "While it wasn't mentioned in the newspaper articles, rumor has it that Abbott and the white man may have been in on it together, and the white man double-crossed him at the last minute."

"What were the trooper's names?" Fargo asked.

Both men shook their heads. Theodore said, "I don't remember seeing their names in the paper. All I recall is troopers."

Earl added, "One of them was the driver."

Fargo grinned. "Are you men saying the Abbott woman's up to something? Hired me to take her on a scouting expedition to find her husband?"

Earl nodded. "Or the other fellow."

Theodore perked up. His eye movements indicated a racing mind. Fargo asked him what he thought. The banker stood and paced next to them. "Earl might have something. Maybe there's substance to those rumors. What if . . ." Theodore's fingers snapped. "That's it," he cried. "She was in on it. Only the lieutenant and the other man kept on going after they stole the payroll." The banker paused and chuckled, "The bastards cut her out, double-crossed her. By now those two are on the West Coast, living high on the hog. I'd bet my bank they are. Sure, she's out looking for them . . . or the money."

Fargo rose, saying, "Only one flaw. The witnesses said the lieutenant was shot up. I don't think I'd forgive and forget such a thing, not even for fifty thousand. But I agree there might be more to it than meets the eye. If there is, I'll find it out soon enough, won't I?"

Grim-faced, they nodded. Fargo swilled his liquor and left the saloon.

He went to the hotel and told the desk clerk he wanted to look at the registration journal. Smiling, she flipped it open for him to read. "There's a chill in the air, big man. You'll need extra warmth tonight."

He barely heard her. All five of the stage passengers had ground-floor rooms, the two men on his side of the hall, the women across from him. He mentally noted their room numbers. Closing the journal, he said, "If I get cold, I'll come looking for you, honey."

"Room sixteen upstairs," she purred. "I'll leave the door unlocked."

He went to his room. Moonlight spilled through the naked window. He checked and found it locked. Sitting on the edge of the bed, he started undressing. Somebody rapped softly on his door. He asked, "Who is it?"

"Me," the brunette answered. "I want to talk to you."

He got up and opened the door. She flung her arms around his neck, raised on tiptoes, and kissed him, openmouthed. He lifted her by the waist and deposited her on the bed. "Damn, what brought that on?" he asked. He sailed his hat to land on top of the bureau, then started taking off his neckerchief.

"Here, let me help with those buttons." She reached for his fly.

He stepped back and looked at her. She was barefoot and had on a thin nightdress that hid nothing. He said, "Honey, I don't sleep with a woman unless I know her name. Aren't you cold?"

"Judith Wells. Yes, I'm cold. That's why I came to visit you. Get over here and warm me up."

He looked past her, to the window, then back at her. "Tell you what. Your bed's probably hotter than mine. Go snuggle down in yours and wait for me. I'll be along in a minute."

"No," she pouted. "If I leave, you'll lock the door. You won't come to me, either."

"Yes, I will. It's just that I need a few minutes alone. Go on. I'll be right behind you."

"Promise? I'll stand in the hall and scream my head off if you don't show up."

"I'll be there."

She came off the bed and embraced him. "And I'll be ready."

After she left, he arranged his bedding to appear as though he was sleeping, then went to Judith's room. He entered without knocking. She had lit the lamp on the little table by her bed. The flimsy nightdress hung from one of the tall posts at the foot of it. She had drawn the covers to just below her eyes. She watched with curiosity as he undressed. She opened the covers for him to join her. He crossed to the bed, his gaze roaming over her body. Her milk-white breasts were larger than he imagined, as were the nipples protruding proudly from her light-brown areolae. She was fleshy but not fat; no bones showed. Her belly was nicely rounded and the button hidden in the wide navel. She'd pulled the covers back far enough to expose most of her dark, curly patch, the top of which began high on her Venus' mound. Gooseflesh covered her skin.

Fargo entered the bed and cupped her right breast. Looking into her eyes, he squeezed firmly and let the nipple poke between his fingers. Judith's breathing quickened. His other hand moved down over her belly, to between her upper thighs. She parted them slightly and writhed to help his middle finger rub high on the slick portal to her inner charms.

She murmured, "Oh, God, yes . . . yes, you're setting me on fire." Her hand gripped and stroked him.

Fargo bent to the breast and rolled the erect nipple between his teeth. She gasped, "Oh, Jesus . . . yes, big man, suck it. Bite me too . . . please, bite me."

As he sucked hard on the nipple and areola, he felt her grip tighten around his member. She whimpered, "Harder, lover . . . more . . . oh, God," and arched her back, encouraging him to take in some of the heavy breast.

Fargo buried his face on the pillowy mound and thrilled her with his lips and tongue. Judith was in constant motion, squirming, arching, breathing rapidly, and mewed, "Get the other one . . . Jesus, yes, suck . . . please."

He accommodated her above and below. The middle finger slipped inside, went deep into her hotness, and began an ever-widening circular motion to prime the love chamber with her hot juices.

She pulled his head back and, gasping, fused her open mouth to his. Their tongues met, circled, and probed deeply. She moaned, "Take me, Fargo . . . take me now."

He rose onto parted knees, sat on his calves, and lifted her onto her knees with her back to him. Her left hand came up and curled around his neck. She arched her back, pressing her tense but parted buttock cheeks against his hard abdomen, and presented her swollen, eager lower lips to his throbbing crown. Gasping, "Now," she raised her hips. He thrust deeply. Judith shrieked, "Oh! Oh! Oh, my God!"

He pushed her facedown on the bed. Gripping her hips, he lifted her rounded ass, came to his knees, and made full penetration. She screamed, "Aaaayeeeiii," grabbed a post on the headboard, and pushed hard. "Oh," she whimpered, "so filling, so hard . . . yes, yes, oh, God, yes . . . faster, big man . . . go faster . . . and deeper. Give it all to me, please. Aaaayeeeiii!"

Fargo lunged twice more, then withdrew and put her on her back. She looked into his lake-blue eyes and smiled, then guided him inside her moist, hot gateway to pleasure. When he went all the way in, she raised her hips and locked her ankles on the small of his back. Together they gyrated in opposite directions to maximize their ecstasy. Judith moaned, "You're turning me to mush in there . . . and I love it. Don't stop . . . oh, please, please, don't stop! Aaaayeeeiii! Jesus, that's so good! I feel it coming! Deeper! Go deeper and harder!"

He felt her ankles unlock and her legs lower. She crossed her legs to tighten her dilated lips around his pounding throbbing member, and arched her back to force in his full length. Her first spasm seized him not unlike a giant hand, and she screamed, "Flood me. Now, Fargo! Set me on fire. Fill me, big man."

Groaning, he erupted in mighty spurts. Her contractions increased in duration and strength, milking him until his scrotum shrank dry. Breathlessly, she confessed, "Jesus, I'll never be the same again. I've never felt this good." Her legs uncrossed and parted wide.

Kissing, they rolled over. Catching his wind, he said, "Honey, you've done this before."

She giggled, "Once or twice, but you brought out the best in me. Can I have more? Please say yes." She love-bit on his chiseled face.

Fargo chuckled. "You women are all alike. You drain us bone-dry, then want to turn us inside out to see if you can find one more drop."

"Well, what's wrong with that? I love being smothered by you. But I guess you've heard that before."

"Once or twice. After I reload, I'll show you how the gypsies do it."

"Take me with you. I'll show you how the French tarts do it. Hell, I'll even show you how the harem girls and the girls from—"

"Whoa," Fargo cut in. What's this 'take me with you' mean?"

"Just that. You are going after the money?"

"Money? What money?"

"She didn't tell you?"

Fargo hedged. "She who? What're you talking about?"

Judith studied his eyes a long moment and tried a smile that didn't work out. She shook her head and said, "I'm sorry. I made a mistake. I thought—"

"Quit thinking," he interrupted, "and get some sleep." He rearranged the pillow and turned on his side to sleep.

Judith left the bed. Seconds later he heard the wooden chair squeak under her weight. A match struck, the bright flare penetrating his drooped eyelids. He squinted one eye when he smelled tobacco smoke. Judith had gotten back in her night clothes and sat with her bare feet on the chair's seat and her knees drawn to her chest. She was staring at him. After a couple of puffs on the ready roll, she asked, "Fargo, are you awake?"

"Unh," he grunted.

"Will you talk to me? Open your eyes and look at me. I don't talk to sleeping men." He opened one eye for her. She said, "I screwed a guy back in Fort Kearny, one of the men on the stagecoach. Everett Liston."

She paused. He waited to hear more about the baritone. "Met him at the saloon where I worked. He was drinking heavily and got all loose-tongued, if you know what I mean."

"And?" Fargo asked when her pause grew lengthy.

"Melody Abbott's husband didn't get shot. Everett said he faked getting shot, and Everett, he told the army so. 'Little darling,' he said to me, 'I got a gut full of lead, and that asshole coward, Lieutenant Julian Abbott, played like he did.' Everett said the officer who questioned him told him to keep his mouth shut about it, that the army would handle things. He said the army wouldn't let the newspaper people talk to him, that everything in the papers was what the army told.

"Another thing. Everett said a white man and a lot of Indians attacked them and stole the payroll wagon he was driving. Said he'd never seen those kind of Indians before. They weren't Cheyenne or Sioux, according to Everett."

Fargo found that interesting.

Judith continued. "Liston is following Melody Abbott. He said she will lead him to the payroll. Hundred thousand dollars, he claims. That's a lot of money. But she doesn't know he's following her. Melody doesn't know him or that he was there when it happened. He saw her once when she visited her husband at Fort Kearny. Everett told me Melody has a—what did he call it—barracks reputation? Anyhow, she has the reputation of being ruthless and pushy, not to mention money-hungry."

Judith uncoiled and stood. He watched her pull on his shirt, then go part the curtains and look out on the street. He waited for her to continue. When she didn't, he probed for more information. "The three men who helped chase off the Cheyenne. While I bandaged the wounded man, I noticed you eyeing them as though you'd seen them before. Had you?"

She looked over her shoulder at him. "You're very observant. Yes, just before boarding the stage in Fort Kearny. When Melody came out of the hotel to board, they came out of the saloon and stood watching her. I mean, watching, as though protecting, not ogling her. I recognize lust when I see it. They didn't view her with lust. Know what I mean?"

"Yeah. Go on."

She waited until she was back under the covers with him. "Fargo, I believe they too are following her. Am I seeing shadows where none exists?"

"Perhaps. On the other hand, if they heard what you did from Liston, your suspicion could be valid. What do you know about the tall blonde, Victoria Ellison?"

"Only that she's looking for a man who double-crossed her: Selman. Her words: 'The sorry bastard left me high and dry.' "

"Did she say what he looked like? Where he might be?"

"No to the last question. Melody also asked her about his looks. Victoria screwed up her face and said he was as rusty as his hair. I didn't understand that. Neither did Melody."

Fargo did. "The other man on the stage? I believe his first name is Sid."

"That's right. Sid Davenport. He didn't have much to say. You know—the quiet type? But he and Everett know each other. It came out when the Cheyenne attacked. Sid looked at Everett and said, 'Jesus, Liston, here we go again!' just like they'd fought Indians before. Something else kinda odd too, now that I think about it. Right after Sid said that, he looked at Victoria. They winked at each other. What do you suppose those winks meant?"

"Beats me, honey. Did they share a bed in Fort Kearny? While you're at it, what do the soldiers at Fort Kearny think happened in regard to that payroll theft?"

"I wouldn't know about them sleeping together, but it's possible. Both had rooms in the hotel. The troopers say Lieutenant Abbott and the other man are hiding out in Indian country, waiting for Melody to join them. Some say Melody came up with the plan. I'm told the two were overheard having a loud argument about the lack of money. She went so far as to say that she was sorry she ever married him, that she didn't want any more of this miserable army life, she deserved better, and so on.

"Anyhow, after the payroll got stolen, the army investigated her. Corporal Willard Simpson told me that. Willard said he was outside the colonel's office when they questioned her, and he heard every word. The colonel had gotten wind of their earlier argument. The army even sent two men to spy on her when she went back home."

"To Kentucky?"

"Kentucky? Yeah, she did say that, didn't she? She lied, Fargo. Melody went back to Cincinnati."

Damn, Fargo thought, how many times does that make I've heard Cincinnati? Judith Wells knows more than she realizes. He asked, "What do you think happened?"

"About the theft?"

"Yes."

She rolled onto him and nuzzled his neck and throat, whispering, "Pretty Melody is on her way to the money, and Liston intends to follow her to it." She slid her palm down his nakedness and gripped his member. Stroking it up, she said, "If you promise to put it back in me, I'll tell you a secret few know about."

Fargo chuckled. "No secret necessary. I planned on doing it anyhow."

She disappeared beneath the covers and started kissing his summit. Between wet kisses, she said, "There's something else the army didn't tell about."

"Oh? What?"

"There was more than a payroll on that wagon. Forty brand-new carbines, plenty of ammunition for them, and ten cases of fine Kentucky bourbon." Her tightened lips drew his foreskin down.

A fusillade of shots, too many, too fast for one revolver, shattered the night . . . and a window across the hall.

3

The walls muted the desk clerk's shriek that filtered down from her room upstairs, but not the louder one from Melody in the room adjacent to Judith's. Judith all but choked on Fargo's manhood.

Fargo pushed her head back. He scooped his gun belt off the night table, dashed out of the room, and ran for the door at the end of the hallway. On the way to it he drew his Colt. He yanked the door open.

The shadowy forms of three horsemen bolted from a cluster of oak well behind the hotel and fled west into the darkness. Fargo emptied the Colt at the riders leaning low over the horse's necks. He heard no telltale sound that any of the five bullets had struck flesh.

He stepped back into the dimly lit hall and checked inside each room. Sid Davenport's was empty. So was Liston's. Neither bed had been slept in. He found Victoria's door locked. He broke it down. She too was gone, although her bed was mussed up.

Backing out the splintered doorway, he collided with somebody and spun to fire. Melody yelped and grabbed his arm to steady herself. He shook his head, saying, "Lady, if I were you, I wouldn't creep up on me again. I could have killed you."

The warning went unquestioned. She asked, "What happened? Who was it?"

He looked past her. The scantily dressed clerk and Theodore, dressed in long johns and gripping his revolver, stood at the lobby end of the hallway. Judith peered out her doorway. All three stared at him.

Melody said impatiently, "I'm waiting, Mr. Fargo."

"Dry-gulchers," he muttered. "Three of them. They're gone, got away clean. You can go back to bed."

Theodore asked, "The bank robbers?"

"Don't know," Fargo replied. "Too dark to see."

Melody glanced at the three open doorways. "Do you think they—"

"Don't know," he repeated, interrupting her. "Could've been."

Judith added, "Or those who helped fight off the Cheyenne."

Fargo said to Melody, "Dawn comes quick, ma'am. I suggest all of us get some sleep."

Her gaze lowered to his groin. She snapped, "Mr. Fargo, I suggest you cover yourself," and went to her room.

He walked around Judith and sat on the edge of the bed to reload the Colt.

She wiggled out of the nightdress, then knelt behind him on the bed and pressed her breasts against his muscled back. Between her nibbles on his neck and shoulders she whispered, "You always make enemies this fast?"

"Sometimes." He chuckled. He holstered the Colt and put the gun belt by the lamp.

Judith's hands came around and grasped his member. "Where was I," she mused, "before we were so rudely interrupted?"

He laid her back and swung his legs onto the bed. "You were about to show me how the harem girls . . ."

Judith Wells bent with her mouth open wide.

Fargo's eyes snapped open and cut to the window. Dawn's first light painted the flimsy curtains. He eased Judith's left arm off his chest and slipped from the bed. Within minutes he was dressed and in the hallway. He went into his room to see what might have been. Shards of glass framed the inside of the window. The bedding was bullet-riddled, shredded. He got his Sharps and gear and left.

Out front he found the crusty driver busy hitching his team to the stagecoach. Fargo paused to give him a hand. "What's your name, old man?" he inquired.

"Lemuel, Lem for short. I heard shooting last night. You kill somebody?"

"They got away clean as a hound's tooth."

"They?"

"Three of them tried to dry-gulch me."

Lem peered over one of the horses. "Goddamn, mister, you must lead a charmed life what with looking down three barrels."

Fargo chuckled. "I wasn't in my bed like they figured I would be."

Lem grinned. "It ain't none of my business, so you can tell me to shut up, but which one of them females had her legs 'round you?"

"Judith Wells. Know her?"

"Oh, sure. Judith's worked all up and down the line. She gets around. The soldier boys at Fort Kearny claim she's the best whore west of the Mississippi. Wouldn't know m'self."

"Do you know why she left Kearny, where she's headed?"

"Her ticket ended right here." Lem glanced up and down the deserted street. "Cain't imagine why, though. Ain't that much business for her here, what with them four saloon girls. Did you get into Judith's past?"

"No," Fargo muttered, "just her—"

Lem's snort stopped him. "It's interesting—her past, I mean."

Fargo waited for him to explain.

Coming around the team, Lem said, "You mean to tell me you ain't heard of Judy Waters?"

Fargo had indeed heard of her. Judy Waters rode with her two older brothers. They robbed banks and held up stages over most of Kansas until caught by a posse. They hanged the brothers, but let her go because of her age. Judy was fourteen.

Theodore's bank flashed to mind. "Reckon she had anything to do with the bank robbery yesterday?"

"Naw," Lem began. "Judy Waters learned her lesson jes' watching 'em give her brothers hemp fever. After that, she changed her name to Judith Wells. But she's always on the lookout for an easy, safe deal. That female's mind is fast as her gun hand. Her being way the hell out here in this nothing place, you can bet she's up to something other than spreading her legs, although she'll damn sure open 'em quick to get what she wants. If you know what I mean."

"Yeah, Lem, I get your drift. Do you know anything about those other two women or the men you brought here?"

"Never saw that one called Victoria afore she showed up at Kearny. I seen Melody Abbott a couple of times. Never talked to her, though. Them soldier boys at Kearny, they say she's mean as a blind rattler. Say her and the lieutenant was having trouble.

"Those two men used to be troopers. Both of 'em was on the payroll detachment what got ambushed . . . if you want to believe that's what happened."

"I take it you do not?"

"That's right. The army never did tell it straight. So what you read ain't necessarily so, an' it damn sure ain't complete."

"Lem, I first heard about that ambush yesterday in the saloon. After I did, I swear that's all I've heard about. What makes you think the army lied?"

"Don't rightly know why they lied, but they did. For one thing, that payroll wagon carried more than money."

It was obvious to Fargo he would have to pry information out of the stage driver. Lem wanted to be asked his opinion. Fargo said, "Uh, huh, that's the second time I've heard that. What else was in the wagon?"

"A small cannon, for one thing. Powder and cannon balls, fourteen boxes of rum, to name a few more. The army never said one word about none of it, or them murdering Shoshoni."

"Shoshoni? Way over here? You sure about that, Lem?"

"Hell, yes, I'm sure. Mister, I was in Laramie when they brung them two wounded, half-dead troopers in. Clear as day, I heard one of 'em scream, 'Shoshoni!' Out of his mind, of course, sweating to beat hell with the fever, but he was still seeing 'em. I could tell by the look in his eyes. They was Shoshoni, all right. Troopers can tell the difference in those savages."

Fargo changed the subject. "Who're you taking to Laramie?"

"Nobody. I'm running empty."

"Charley?"

"Naw, he ain't fit to travel. Buck Thorne's riding shotgun for me. Glad you mentioned Charley, though."

Fargo watched him open the stage door and reach inside. Lem brought out a big, fleece-lined coat that he handed to him, saying it belonged to Charley. "He asked me to give it to you. Might say it's Charley's way of thanking you for what you did for him."

Fargo pulled the coat on. It felt warm and fit perfectly.

Lem continued. "Said he ain't gonna need it no more. Charley's going back to Louisiana and take up farming again. He's had all the frontier he wants."

Fargo nodded. "Tell him I said thanks and I hope he heals fast. Old-timer, you take care." Fargo headed for the livery.

Lem shouted, "I'd keep one eye cocked on her if I was you!"

Fargo walked inside the livery and went to his pinto. A stable boy no older than twelve was cleaning out stalls. After dumping a spadeful of manure outside, the boy moseyed over and said, "Mighty purdy black-and-white stallion you got there, mister. Two men already tried to buy it from Mr. Coble. One came in after the bank was held up and the other later on."

Fargo snugged the cinch before looking at the young-ster. "Did they, now? What did Mr. Coble say?"

The boy waited to reply until he climbed up to sit on

one side of the stall. "He told 'em it wasn't for sale. They bought two others, the dappled gray mare and dun gelding. One of the women took the Appaloosa mare. The other bought that black stallion over there."

Fargo followed his point to a stall across the alley-way. The horse stood at least seventeen hands. Takes a helluva woman to handle a horse that size, he thought.

The youngster lamented, "Gonna miss that 'Paloosa mare, I am. I wanted that horse real bad."

"A woman bought it, huh? What did she look like?"

"Didn't see her buy it. I was over at the general store visiting my friends, Tom and Erlene. Their folks own the store. Mr. and Mrs. Bentley, they had a good day too. Those same two men and women bought rifles, bedrolls, and everything from 'em."

"Did any of them mention where they're headed?" He strapped the saddlebags and bedroll in place.

"Mrs. Bentley, she's nosy. She right out asked. Only one I heard answer her was the tall woman. And all she said was west. That's a Tom-fool thing for a woman to do all by herself, ain't it, mister?"

The lad was full of information.

Fargo nodded and inserted the Sharps in its saddle case.

Melody walked inside and headed for the black stallion. She wore new Levi's, black riding boots, a buckskin shirt, and a wide-brimmed hat. Her arms were loaded down with things for the journey; bedroll, bulging saddlebags, and a Spencer .52. She started making the stallion ready to ride.

Fargo said, " 'Morning."

She ignored him.

The boy hopped to the ground and went to help her.

She pushed him away, barking, "I'll do it. That way I'll know it's done correctly."

The youngster shrugged and came to lean on the stall gate with Fargo. They watched her finish with the stallion, then back it out into the alleyway. She climbed into the saddle, flicked narrowed eyes at Fargo, and snapped, "I'm ready, Mr. Fargo. Let's go."

Fargo eased into his saddle. In a no-nonsense tone, he told her, "We have a long ride ahead of us. I don't want to hear you bite at me another time. From now on, you follow my rules, obey me without question. Don't, and I'll let the Indians take you and sew up your mouth. Do I make myself clear?"

She spurred the horse to move out. Over her shoulder she said, "I'll do what you say, Mr. Fargo, short of letting you maul me like you obviously did that hussy last night. You should be ashamed of yourself, running around naked when proper ladies are present."

Fargo shot the boy a wink and nudged the Ovaro into a walk. He was halfway through the wide entrance when several shots cracked the still air. The slugs buzzed past his head and tore into the far wall. He instantly backed the Ovaro into the livery, dismounted, and drew his Colt.

The boy hollered, "Over yonder, mister. They're behind the bath fence."

Melody raced inside and slid from the saddle, bringing the Spencer with her. She sprinted to Fargo and asked, "What do you want me to do? They're across the street."

The boy said, "Mister, there's a hole in the back wall big 'nuff for you to get through. Want me to show it to you?"

"Yes." He told Melody, "When you hear me yell, 'Now,' stick your rifle around the corner and start shooting toward the fence."

She nodded. He followed the kid to the hole. Fargo crawled through it and hurried around the building to the street corner. None of the gunmen was visible to him. The board fence, like everything else on that side of the street, was still bathed in dark shadows. Fargo wanted a target. He yelled, "Now!"

The Spencer roared. Muzzle flashes from return fire winkled from wide gaps in fence. Fargo muttered,

"Aw, shit," and opened fire. His slugs chewed a tight pattern in one of the planks. A high-tenor voice yelped, "Ow," then shouted, "He's at the corner."

Four bullets instantly dug into the wood next to Fargo's face. The Spencer answered them. Fargo reloaded and squatted to peer around the corner. After a few silent seconds, he heard hoofbeats pounding west from the far side of the bath area. He ran into the street and waited for the riders to come into view. They emerged riding close together, bent low over their mounts, the tails of their dusters flying in the wind. Distant and indistinct though they were, Fargo fired till the hammer fell on a spent casing.

Melody came onto the street and took a long shot at them. She missed also. He walked to her. She asked, "Did you see who they were?"

"No."

"Were they the same ones as last night?"

"Might've been."

"You aren't very observant, are you, Mr. Fargo? I believe I would pay more attention if somebody were trying to kill me."

"Get on that horse and follow me by four or five lengths." Fargo had all of the mouthy woman he could stand. "Make it ten lengths. I don't want to hear your voice the rest of this day."

Fuming, she drew her lips thin and strode back inside the livery. He whistled for the Ovaro. It trotted up to him, its ears perked. He swung up into the saddle and headed west. As he had told her, Melody followed at ten lengths.

Within the hour Fort Hope disappeared from sight. They rode in raw open country with the unseen North Platte far to their left. The rolling landscape offered little to view but dried sage and prairie grass. In the low places carved by millennia of runoffs from rainfalls grew pine sanctuaries for birds, including wild turkey, which the Sioux never ate. They had long ago determined the turkey was nature's absolute stupidest fowl. They feared its stupidity would be contagious.

Fargo knew the foothills of the Siouan's most sacred Paha Sapa—the Black Hills—forbidden to white men under threat of immediate death, were beyond the rises on their right. A long series of cliffs rose straight ahead.

Coming near the cliffs, he heard thunder rumbling on top of them and reined to a halt. Melody rode up and broke her silence. "What is it, Mr. Fargo? Can't be thunder, although it certainly sounds like it. There's not one cloud in the sky."

"Buffalo," he muttered. "Be quiet and listen. You'll hear what stampeded them."

The rumble grew louder. When it reached a crescendo, obviously about to spill over the cliffs, they heard Indians yelling, *"Ho-kah! Ho-kah!"*

Suddenly, the leading edge of a buffalo herd hurtled over the rim of the cliff. Melody's hands raised to her mouth to trap a cry. Mesmerized, she watched dozens of bison crash and die at the bottom of the cliff. When the rest of the herd turned away, the rumble began to fade. Mounted Sioux warriors appeared on the edge of the cliff to survey their kill.

Fargo explained, "Doesn't always work out because there's not always a cliff nearby. But when there is and enough buffalo are close at hand, it's easier and much less dangerous for the hungry Sioux to stampede them over the cliff. Watch in that draw over there." He pointed at the depression that ran from the top of the cliff to its base. "In a minute you'll see Indian women file down it and go to the buffalo. They'll be here till sunset, skinning and butchering. They leave nothing."

"The bones? Surely they have no use for the bones."

"Some of them. Certain ribs are used in making saddles for women. Other bones find their way into the women's households. I suppose I should say, tepeeholds. You see, the tepee belongs to the woman. It's her job to make them. The warriors role is to provide and protect. She cuts down and peels the poles, tans and sews together the buffalo hides to make the covering. She puts up her tepee and strikes it. He sits and watches."

"That's terrible."

"Not if you're Sioux. Their society is more orderly than the white man's. Come on. We'll ride up and see if they'll invite us to dinner."

She gasped, "Eat with savages? Never, Mr. Fargo!"

He didn't answer. Instead, he rode forward.

4

Fargo approached the Sioux women slowly while keeping his eyes on the warriors watching from atop the cliff. Melody followed closely. He motioned her to move alongside.

When the black stallion was beside him, he said, "We're now in their territory. It's important we follow their ways and customs. This means both of us must do things that do not apply back in Fort Hope or beyond. I know the abrupt change will be difficult for you to accept, but you must at least try. Come the dawn, we'll be gone. Have you played follow-the-leader?"

She cleared her throat, the only indication of her tension, and said, "As a child, yes. But I—"

"No buts to it," Fargo interrupted. "Listen to me and you will get through the night with no problem. Argue with me and you'll wish you hadn't.

"First and foremost, be sure you get in your head that the males dominate, or at least appear to." He paused, expecting her to challenge the warning. When she didn't, he picked up on his survival lecture. "Do not—I repeat, do not—make eye contact with any man, not even me, unless we are alone."

"Fargo, you're asking me to—"

"Shut up, Melody," he cut in caustically, "and listen. Anytime a woman looks a man in the eye, these people take it either as a sign of disrespect or as an invitation to sex. Watch and you will notice none of these women will look me in the eye. Out of training and habit, they will keep their eyes lowered. On the other hand, if I were to make a move on one or threaten them in any way, they will not only look at me, they will also defend themselves most vigorously, because of my obvious disrespect for females. You can look at other women, but for your own good, don't look at the men."

"What if I accidentally—"

Again he cut her off. "You won't. Here's why. If you do, you have to pay a penalty. I'll have to beat you while they watch."

"You wouldn't," she gasped.

"Yes, I would. Count on it, and you won't accidentally make a slip. Also, Melody, don't speak unless you're spoken to. Even then make it brief and without emotion. One final thing. Back to follow-the-leader. Practice the three L's; look, listen, and learn. Pay attention to what happens around you. These people don't play games. They don't have time for that. There's a good reason for everything they do. Act accordingly and they will accept you. Think you can remember those few things?"

"Of course. However, what if one of the men . . . you know, tries to force himself on me? I won't accept that."

"That's the one thing that won't happen. You're with me. They will automatically presume you are my woman."

Her long sigh evidenced her great relief.

After a moment Fargo said, "The Sioux do not practice materialism, neither are they greedy people. Yet they give things and dearly love to receive gifts. What you would call tokens are treasures to them. Is there anything in your saddlebags you might give away?"

"How about my earrings?"

"Earrings are perfect. Before we leave, give them to the woman whose tepee you stayed in. And, Melody, whatever she gives you in return, fawn over it. Make her feel good."

They halted near the dead buffalo. As he had said, the women kept their eyes on skinning and butchering activities. Fargo waited for warriors to come down and check out the two *wah-see-shoo*, white people.

Six of them astride ponies came down the draw and halted among the women to face Fargo and Melody. She stared at her saddle horn. He reminded himself to compliment her the first chance he got. The Trailsman spoke Lakota to the warriors. "Hello, my friends. I see you have had a good hunt today. My mouth waters to taste of it. We come in peace, my red brothers." He held out his Colt and Sharps by their barrels to prove it.

A muscular warrior nudged his pony forward and took both weapons. After looking them over, he handed them back and said, "Welcome, friend. Yes, today we have plenty to eat. We must remain to protect the women. I will have Running Bear take you to our encampment to sit with our headman, Swift Water." Using sign language, the warrior told those on the cliff to lead Fargo to Swift Water and say they were friends.

Fargo said, *"Pilamaya."*

The warrior nodded.

Fargo glanced at Melody, still gazing at the horn, and said, "When I finish talking, dismount and start helping the women." He saw her eyes widen, her body stiffen. "Don't you dare utter one word, Melody Abbott. I know you don't know anything about what they are doing. Before this day is over, you will. They're taking me to meet the headman. I'll see you there." He handed her his throwing knife. "Don't leave it behind, ma'am." He reined the pinto right and spurred it to walk. As he left, he heard Melody groan and dismount. He also heard the warrior mutter, *"Washtay. Lee-lah wash-tay."*

Yes, Fargo thought, it is good, very good for her. Perhaps a few hours of working in blood will make the arrogant woman more tolerable, toughen her to survive the ordeals that always crop up unexpectedly on long trips such as this one. He spurred the Ovaro up the draw.

A half-naked warrior waited at the top. Fargo looked at the brawny young man whom he guessed might be in his late teens and said, "Greetings. My name is Skye Fargo."

The warrior smiled. *"Lee-lah wash-tay.* You speak my language. Come, white man. We can talk while riding. I have much to ask. My name is Running Bear."

The rode north for at least two miles. True to his word, Running Bear asked many questions, most of them about the white man's ways. He could not imagine tall buildings or that people worked and lived in them. He had no concept of money or outhouses. Fargo learned they were going to a large encampment of Sioux from the Sans Arc band.

Riding into the camp, Fargo counted nineteen tepees. Running Bear led him through the encampment, and Fargo noted the virtual absence of women. A few, too old to handle the work demanded by on-site slaughtering of buffalo, watched over children at play. Others sat in dark shadows inside tepees and watched the white stranger momentarily before moving completely out of sight. Running Bear halted in front of a tepee with its lower part painted black. When he hopped off the pony, Fargo dismounted.

Running Bear stood next to the entrance to announce their arrival. "Grandfather, it is I, Running Bear, who comes. We had a good hunt, Grandfather. Two white people were there. They come in peace, Grandfather. The man speaks our language. He is with me. His woman helps our women."

After a moment of silence a mellow voice spoke from within. *"Wash-tay.* You may enter, Running Bear. Bring him to me."

Without being told Fargo removed his boots and set them outside by the door flap. He followed the warrior inside.

They sat facing Chief Swift Water across a small fire. Except for two rawhide thongs looped around his neck, the old man was naked from the waist up.

Running Bear said, "Grandfather, his name is Skye Fargo."

Swift Water glanced up. "Are you the man called the Trailsman?"

"Yes, Grandfather," Fargo answered, relieved that his other Sioux brothers had mentioned him in favorable light.

"*Lee-lah wash-tay*. My relatives, Hunkpapa and Oglala, told me about a big white man who spoke Lakota and knew their ways. Your woman is helping with the kill?"

"Yes, Grandfather. Although I'm afraid she may be more in the way than of help. It's her first time."

The old man nodded and chuckled softly. "Our women might skin her. But it is good she offered to help. You will stay in camp and share the feast with us. We will powwow. You have been in the sweat lodge?"

"Yes, Grandfather, many times."

"*Wash-tay*. You and your woman will sweat and pray with us this night." He looked at Running Bear. "When the hunting party returns, bring Long Nose to me." His gaze shifted onto Fargo. "Your woman will stay in Long Nose's tepee. His women will take care of her needs. You will stay with Running Bear and his woman." Again he looked at the young warrior. "Take our friend to Crazy Fire."

Running Bear grunted, "Yes, Grandfather. What if Crazy Fire sleeps? Am I to—"

The old man's raised hand and hard stare stopped the forming question. A wave of the hand dismissed the issue of whether or not Crazy Fire slept and the two men sitting across from him. Swift Water added another stick of firewood to the flickering flames.

The young man put his foot in the bucket that time, Fargo thought. He might make another mistake, but not that one again. He preceded Running Bear through the opening.

They went to Crazy Fire's tepee. Running Bear rapped on the tepee covering several times and said, "It is I, Running Bear. I have—"

A gruff voice cut him short of explaining. "Go away, Running Bear, or I'll put bad medicine on you."

Grim-jawed, the young warrior remarked, "And you will have Swift Water to answer to. He sent me."

The door flap parted. A fat face with narrowed eyes appeared. They glanced from the warrior to Fargo. "Who, what have we here? A captive?" He sounded hopeful.

"No," Running Bear began. "He is the Trailsman, Skye Fargo, our friend. Swift Water told me to bring him to you."

"Why?" Crazy Fire grunted, more to himself than to them for the explanation.

"I don't know," Running Bear said, obviously irritated. "He and his woman are to sweat and pray with us tonight. Perhaps—"

Crazy Fire motioned them inside. Upon entering the tepee, Fargo knew Crazy Fire was the medicine man. His garb—a cougar skin complete with the head intact—hung from a pole behind him. The cougar's mouth gaped full open, the lips drawn back to bare the flesh-ripping teeth. It had no eyes, only sockets painted bright yellow. Two gourd rattles mounted on the ends of foot-long pieces of slim chokecherry limbs dangled from the same pole. On the other ends of the limbs were eagle's feet, the black talons opened to seize.

The fact Crazy Fire sat with his back to his visitors told Fargo the medicine man was also *hay-oh-kah*. He probably did most everything contrary to the norm. Fargo had seen *hay-oh-kahs* ride facing the pony's rear end, others who entered the blistering hot sweat lodge dressed for blizzards. They did most everything backward. Fargo had also discovered they were invariably smart.

Crazy Fire calmly announced, "I shall heat fifty stones tonight. One for each of us in the circle, the rest for them. The whites will sizzle, fry, and beg to get out. I won't let them. I won't even call for the door between rounds. Tell him that, Running Bear."

Running Bear cleared his throat and said, "Crazy Fire, he speaks and understands our language."

The fat glob hardly flinched.

Fargo wedged into the discussion. "Crazy Fire honors us with so few stones. I thank you for being considerate. Will one or more or your women sweat with us?"

Crazy Fire visibly stiffened. "Yes," he answered. "Running Bear will pick a woman. Go now and let me pray neither of you will perish."

Outside, Running Bear suggested Melody suddenly become too ill to sweat. "He's crazy, Skye Fargo. Not even I can sweat fifty stones without the door being opened. He will kill her. You too."

"No," Fargo said, "she sweats. She has to. Your chief ordered it."

Running Bear grimaced and shook his head balefully.

They walked to his tepee without further discussion on the matter. After ushering Fargo inside, Running Bear apologized for having to leave him. "I must return to my brothers," he said. "We will be back before the sun goes to sleep."

Fargo nodded and started pulling off his clothes. The warrior made one final plea before departing. "Swift Water will understand if she goes to the moon tepee."

Fargo shook his head and repeated, "No, she sweats," and added, "or dies in the trying. She must be subjected to the sweat. Later, we may meet other *tiospayes* and be tested in their lodges. She needs to know what happens."

Running Bear nodded and left. Fargo stretched out on the buffalo robe and went to sleep.

The plod of many horses coming into Swift Water's camp vibrated the ground. Fargo's eyes snapped open. He rolled onto his back and looked through the upper draft opening. Twin feathery clouds arched east to west high in the peach-colored sky. Heaven's brighter stars would soon appear.

Fargo yawned, stretched, and sat to look out the lower portal. Mounted warriors preceded the long line of women on foot. One of the warriors trailed the black stallion burdened with a buffalo carcass. Fargo looked beyond it to spot Melody.

She trudged next to a woman near the middle of the slow-moving column. Like most of the other women—dog-tired from hard work followed by a lengthy hike—her chin touched her collarbone. Melody carried a hind-quarter. Her walking partner's arms cradled a furry buffalo head. Like all the others, her clothes were blood-soaked.

Fargo pulled on his clothes and went outside to watch the procession. Running Bear rode to him and slid off his pony. The man was caked with dirt and dust. Fargo reached inside the opening and fetched the buffalo stomach hanging on a tepee pole and filled with water.

Running Bear took it eagerly and drank his fill. Returning the water bag, he said, "Your woman works hard, Skye Fargo. She has a fast knife. Come, we will clean our bodies while the women complete their work."

Running Bear took him to a large spring-fed pond nestled among the stand of whispering pine north of the campsite. As he undressed, Fargo scanned the peaceful setting. Warriors were hitching their ponies to a long rope stretched between two pines downstream of the gurgling creek. A sweat lodge stood near the west bank of the pond. Fargo couldn't see the lodge door, which meant it was on the west side of the dome-shaped structure—contrary, like its builder. The absence of a slightly smaller lodge meant this medicine man sweated men and women together, which was also contrary to the norm.

After hitching their ponies, the warriors hurried to the pond. Several acknowledged Fargo with quick nods, others grunted, "Unh," while a few said, "*Hau, mi kola.*"

He returned the amenities in kind, then eased a foot into the icy water, shivered, and stiff as a board, fell face-first. He came up gasping. A chorus of laughter echoed through the woods. Fargo had been accepted.

Now the warriors posed many questions for him to answer. Most concerned Melody, whom they'd obviously watched with fascination. One asked, "Whose camp did you steal her from?" Another said, "She worked hard." The chubby warrior floating next to him added, "Some of our women could not keep up with your woman."

And so it went until the cool late October evening air chased them out of the water. As he dressed, Fargo heard shrieks and giggles erupt downstream. Running Bear explained, "The women have finished with the buffalo meat. After a hunt they wash below, where the ponies drink. Do you powwow, Skye Fargo?"

"Yes, I have danced in the circle with Lakota. Your Brule relatives."

"Good." Running Bear smiled.

They walked side by side back to camp, where the older women, with much help from young girls, were busy preparing the feast. The aroma of roasting buffalo meat was carried in the haze of smoke from numerous cooking fires. Fargo inhaled deeply.

They crossed a large open area surrounded by te-pees. Two warriors stood watching four old women stack long pieces of firewood in the center of the clearing. An oversize drum stood on the southern perimeter. Shortly the wood would blaze high, and the throaty sound of the drum would throb in the night air.

Rounding a tepee, they saw a muscular warrior bent to enter it. He glanced at them, then raised upright. His unusually long nose foretold his name. "*Hau*, Long Nose. This is our *ko-lah*, Skye Fargo. Swift Water said his woman will share your tepee."

Long Nose grunted, "Unh." Fargo detected displea-sure in the guttural sound. Long Nose asked, "How long do I keep the white woman?"

Fargo answered, "Overnight. We leave with the rising sun."

Long Nose grunted, *"Wash-tay,"* and stepped inside the tepee.

Running Bear shrugged. They continued on to his tepee.

While Fargo made a small fire to knock off the night

chill, Running Bear unrolled a bulging buckskin bundle that held his dance costume. Fargo sat and watched his newfound friend stand and shake wrinkles from his costume, which was in keeping with his name: a wide band of quills overlaid the tunic made of black bear skin that hung to his thighs. The red sash served as a belt, and knee-high leggings, also furry black bear, matched the moccasins. Running Bear held up a necklace of bear claws for Fargo to see and marvel at.

Fargo told him, *"Lee-lah wash-tay,"* for the craftsmanship was very good indeed.

Two young women came through the opening. Both glanced down instantly after seeing the white stranger. Fargo spoke to Running Bear, although the women heard every word. "You can tell them I will not be offended if they look at me."

Running Bear considered his statement a moment, then told them they could look and speak to Fargo inside the tepee, but nowhere else. They visibly relaxed and moved to lounge on buffalo robes spread opposite the opening. Running Bear made the introductions. Puckering toward the slimmer female, he said, "Her name is Dancing Cloud." Shifting the pucker at the shorter and stockier, he said, "Happy Flower is my mate." Looking at Fargo, he said, "This is the Trailsman, Skye Fargo, our friend. Skye Fargo, Dancing Cloud will share your robes tonight."

Fargo knew better than to insult his host by objecting or rejecting. Running Bear, obedient to custom and the act of giving, had given Dancing Cloud to him. Dancing Cloud had no voice in the matter. Fargo suspected Running Bear welcomed being relieved of the woman if only for one night. Happy Flower more or less confirmed it when she smiled, formed a circle with her thumb and index finger, and poked her other index finger through the circle. She mumbled, "Dancing Cloud likes big warriors."

Dancing Cloud smiled weakly. But Fargo saw her eyes lower onto his crotch. He asked, "Did my woman do a good job?"

Both females nodded. Happy Flower said, "She sweated a lot. What does 'goddamn' mean, white man?"

Fargo could not help laughing. The buffalo had broken Melody's uppity crust and exposed much about her. Fargo replied, "That means I'm tired and I want to go home."

The women giggled behind their hands. Dancing Cloud suggested, "Then she will not mind my"—she duplicated Happy Flower's finger movements, only more vigorously, and completed the hanging sentence—"with you?"

Fargo commented, "No, she will not mind. She will be grateful. In fact, Melody will be extremely pleased. And so will I." He could already feel Dancing Cloud's long slim legs wrapped around his waist.

Through an easy, knowing grin, Running Bear told the women to go find firewood for their tepee fire. As they were leaving, he added, "And see if the powwow fire burns and the drummers are there."

Fargo asked for the order of the feast events. Running Bear answered, "We eat while we rest from dancing. Swift Water will say when to sweat. Watch Crazy Fire. When he leaves the powwow, that is the signal to prepare yourself. I will take you to the sweat lodge."

"Melody?"

"I will have one of our women bring her."

A slow beating of the drum meant the meat was ready and it was time to begin dancing. Fargo stripped to the waist. Running Bear put on his costume. The two women returned, removed their buckskin dresses, and stood naked while they pulled out special dresses and shawls.

To Fargo's pleasure, Dancing Cloud presented small but well-formed breasts—the dark nipples were quite large, the paler areolae unusually small—slim work-hard buttock cheeks, and a splendid patch of pubic hair that glistened blue-black. He was aroused instantly.

Fully dressed now, Running Bear tapped him on the shoulder with the coup stick and broke his reverie. "Shall we go?" he asked.

Fargo rose to follow him outside.

The tempo of the drumbeat quickened, and with it the singers commenced a high-pitched song, through which one voice shrilled mightily. The hair on Fargo's nape perked. He tingled all over and found his feet already moving in the Lakota two-step, ready to dance.

Running Bear preceded him into the circle: the women danced in a loose group at its east end, and the men moved around it sunwise. Energetic children danced wherever they pleased. And practically everybody did dance. Those who didn't tended to the cooking meat or stood behind the six drummers and sang along with them while bouncing in rhythm.

Crazy Fire was the first to drop out. Fargo presumed dancing backward and in the opposite direction was unusually tiring for the obese medicine man. Crazy Fire plopped down between the drum and dancers and motioned for one of the old women to bring him food and drink. She scuttled off to obey. One simply did not argue with a *heyoka.*

Fargo was enjoying himself until he saw Melody Abbott staring at him through squinted eyes. Her lips were drawn thin. He expected her tongue to dart out at him any second. She sat cross-legged with two other nondancing women on the sidelines near the drummers. All held hunks of cooked meat. He arched his eyebrows and smiled at her. She brought the piece of meat to her mouth and gnawed on it viciously, as though saying, "I wish this were your throat!"

Swift Water danced out of the circle and sat cross-legged beside Crazy Fire. The downward folding movement was done gracefully and easily, attesting he'd done it a thousand or more times. A woman handed him a gourd dipper of water, then waited for him to drink it dry before she handed him a small roast.

Fargo moved to the perimeter across from the drum. Running Bear danced out of the circle and joined him. Between breaths he said, "I'm tired, Skye Fargo, and hungry and thirsty. Let us go find food and water."

Fargo nodded and followed the make-believe black

bear to a spit nearby. The woman tending it carved two big pieces from the huge roast and handed them to the man-bear and the white man. They ate as they walked toward a large water bag suspended from a tripod lodgepole pine. As Running Bear guzzled down four dippers of water, Fargo wondered aloud, "I saw your medicine man get up and walk backward toward the North Star."

"Yes, I too noticed. He crammed a whole buffalo in his mouth. We will dance the next one, then go."

They returned as the lead drummer made the downbeat. Dancing into the circle, Fargo looked beyond the bonfire to see how Melody was doing. She wasn't there. Swift Water had also left the powwow. Concerned and eager to have the sweat over so he could lie down, Fargo was grateful when the dance ended.

He and Running Bear went to the tepee to undress and prepare for the sweat. Running Bear asked, "Did you warn your woman, tell her what to expect?" His eyes widened, signaling a sudden, new thought.

Fargo anticipated the forming question and answered it. "No, I haven't talked to her since we came to the slaughter. I don't know if she understands the sweat. We never discussed it."

Visibly uneasy, Running Bear suggested, "Then tell her, Skye Fargo. Once inside, Crazy Fire will not let her out until all the water is poured. If she screams, somebody will close her mouth and hold her down until it is over. Warn her, please."

"I will," Fargo conceded, "right before we crawl in."

No more was said as they prepared for the sweat lodge. Neither did they discuss the matter en route.

5

The sweat fire containing the conical stack of stones fairly roared. Its flames licked high. Sparkling orange-red embers were carried in the updraft.

Crazy Fire sat on a stump with his back to the fire he had made. He was dressed to survive a raging blizzard. Fargo wondered if he was still devouring meat.

Swift Water sat cross-legged and alone. He'd already undressed. His coal-black eyes stared into the fire, his much-wrinkled face a study in immobility, wisdom, and serenity.

Long Nose stood with three warriors, two of whom leaned on handles of pitchforks made from elk antlers. They too studied the fire. One of the warriors would handle the door flap, opening and closing it on command by Crazy Fire. The other warrior would tend the fire.

A hefty young girl of no more than thirteen stood nearby, gazing at the star-studded, ink-black sky. Her presence meant she was still innocent and, as such, would move the stones from the fire to inside the lodge. Fargo heard one of the warriors call her Many Laughs.

Melody Abbott was fully dressed. She sat on the ground at the side of the lodge, her eyes transfixed on the fire. A woman about her age and height, only heavier, stood nearby with her arms folded across her bosom. She too was fully dressed. Both females appeared very tired—exhausted, in fact. Melody didn't notice Fargo and Running Bear walk into the glow of the fire and join Long Nose, or if she did she ignored them.

The one word, *"Hoka,'* "let's go," uttered by Crazy Fire triggered the statuelike assemblage into motion.

The warriors holding the elkhorn pitchforks stepped to the fire and started pulling away the long pieces of flaming firewood to expose the pyramid of white-hot, almost-transparent stones.

Long Nose removed his buckskin apron and pitched it on top of the lodge.

The girl moved closer to the fire pit.

Fargo and Running Bear started undressing.

Swift Water uncoiled effortlessly and emptied his bladder on a clump of dry buffalo grass.

Melody stiffened and inspected her fingers.

Crazy Fire heaved his bulk from the stump and waddled backward toward the scant entrance to the sweat lodge.

Fargo wondered how in the world the fat man would squirm inside. As though sucked in by magic, Crazy Fire simply disappeared into the black maw.

One of the warriors handed his pitchfork to the girl, then shed his clothes and crawled inside.

Running Bear glanced at Fargo, his expression pleading for him to hurry and warn his woman, then dropped onto hands and knees and crawled in, muttering, *"Me-tock-we-ahs-ee."*

Fargo stepped in front of Melody. He lifted her by the armpits. She looked up quickly and opened her mouth to spew God only knew what at him. He clamped a hand over her mouth and literally dragged her behind the dome and out of earshot of those inside it. In a low but deadly serious voice he said, "If you won't scream or speak, I'll remove my hand." She hesitated before nodding.

He took the hand away and continued. "I don't like this any more than you, but Swift Water has ordered us to participate in this purification rite with him. If we refuse, he will be insulted greatly, and God only knows what will happen to us. Death for me, a living hell for you, in all probability. Nod if you understand."

She exhaled mightily before nodding reluctantly. He said, "Remember, Melody, anything they can do, we can do. We are going to crawl back inside our Mother Earth's womb, symbolically, of course, where we were safe and secure, where it was warm and moist . . . and we were naked."

That was too much for Melody to choke down. Fargo quickly returned his hand to her mouth and hissed, "Woman, listen to me. Nothing is going to happen to you. Nobody will touch you. Once that flap comes down, it will be so dark in there nobody can see you, or you them. They are not in there to lust for your body. If they wanted your body, they'd have already had it dozens of times. You're the one who wanted, insisted, on making this trip. Well, this lodge is in our path. One final thing, and then you start peeling off those clothes."

She bit his finger. He jerked his hand back. She whispered, "What?"

"You will think the heat in there is insufferable. Just remember they're sitting in it too. Don't you dare scream or beg for mercy. Those are signs of weakness, and bad things happen quick to weak people. Savvy?"

"What if I faint?"

"Fine. I suggest you try. Oh, I forgot one thing. Again play follow-the-leader. I'll be seated on your right. Everything moves from right to left. Listen to what is said, and you'll know what to say when it comes your turn. Now, I see Swift Water is waiting patiently for us to enter. So shuck those clothes, scoot in, and crawl left to the back of the lodge. I'll be right behind you."

"You'll look at my—"

"Honey, what have you got that I haven't seen mountains and valleys of before? That girl, Many Laughs, is the only virgin in this crowd. So take off your clothes or I'll tear them off."

Melody Abbott, with her eyes downcast, staring

disgustedly at the ground, pulled off her clothes and sprinted to the door. She hesitated to drop onto hands and knees until Fargo bumped into her backside. She flinched, closed her eyes, and followed the now-nude other woman inside. Fargo had to grab her foot to stop her at the back of the lodge.

Swift Water uttered, *"Me-tock-we-ahs-ee,"* and crawled inside and sat next to the door.

Everybody except Crazy Fire sat facing the pit in the center of the lodge, where the hot stones would be put. Being contrary, he sat with his back to the pit. Fargo wondered how he would manage to pour the water without turning around, and concluded he would turn, once total darkness consumed the interior. Crazy Fire beckoned for the virgin to start bringing the stones.

Fargo counted fifty-six—twice the number of ribs in their sacred buffalo. All were the size of Crazy Fire's head. Next came half a large geode filled with water and a buffalo horn to pour with. The flap was lowered, sealing them in. Heat built up rapidly. Contrary to what Fargo told Melody, they could clearly see everything from the searing-hot glow of the stones.

The rocks sizzled and spat angrily when Crazy Fire poured four horns of water onto them without turning around.

Melody's groans were lost in the loud song that called in the spirits and began with the fourth pouring. The song asked the spirits to hear and honor their prayers. Fargo, wise in the ways of sweating in an Indian lodge with a small mountain of lava-hot rocks, bent his head between his knees and touched his nose and lips to the bed of sage that covered the ground around the stone pit. The cooling effect gave instant relief from the dense cloud of steam trapped inside the dome.

Fargo added his voice to the prayerful song and the next two that followed swiftly, as though all three were a medley. Crazy Fire poured four times at the beginning of each song. After the twelve horns of water, the mound of stones still glowed bright orange-red, although the glow was greatly diffused in the steam.

During the third song, Fargo felt Melody's lips searching for his left ear. Her soft hands cupped it when the tender moist lips found the ear. She whispered in hot gasps, "I can't take any more of this. Get me out of here, please. My heart is ready to pound out of my chest. Please, Mr. Fargo, please."

He cupped her right ear and whispered, "No, Melody, I can't. Lie facedown behind me. Bury your face in the sage. Be very still, ignore the heat and think of something cold, such as a creek."

Her limp body collapsed against him. He picked up on the song while he gently laid her behind him.

As he'd promised, Crazy Fire did not call for the door to be opened after the first round of songs. Instead, they sat silent for the few minutes normally allowed for the door flap to be raised so most of the steam would escape and be replaced by cool, fresh air.

The fat medicine man grunted for Swift Water to start the prayer round. When the old headman muttered, "O Great Spirit," the stones spat from a hornful of water. Swift Water continued without pause, "Swift Water prays to you. Great Spirit, I pray for wisdom."

For what seemed an eternity, those sitting in the circle listened to less than two minutes of Swift Water's outpourings for wisdom to lead and judge fairly. At the end of his prayer he muttered, *"Me-tock-we-ahs-see,"* signaling he was through, and the warrior on his left could begin.

More water was poured as the warrior commenced praying. His lengthy, sometimes wandering prayer, focused on the neighboring Crow, long-standing enemies of the Sioux and Shoshoni. The warrior begged for the Crow to be strong in battle, for he and his Sans Arc brothers did not want an easy or cheap victory. When he uttered the standard closing, which meant "all my relations," Fargo raised his head and spoke, referring to the Great Spirit by the venerated name Grandfather.

"O Great Spirit, it is I, Skye Fargo, a pitiful human being, who comes suffering, praying to you." Six, not four, horns of water drenched the rocks and sizzled. "Grandfather, as always I first pray that all people will live long lives, be healthy, happy, and reasonably prosperous."

Swift Water and Running Bear grunted, "Unh," to indicate they heard and appreciated that consideration.

Fargo continued. "Great Spirit, I pray for vision to see into the future. I am on a long journey to where the sun lowers each day into the great waters that have no end. I must pass through other red lands, Great Spirit, the Crow's and Shoshoni's first. I beg you, Grandfather, to let me see in advance the way through, the way that will cause no harm to me or my red brothers, for I come in peace, Great Spirit. Please show me where to go. *Me-tock-we-ahs-ee.*"

Water hit and exploded into steam. To Fargo's surprise but great pleasure, Melody began a prayer, speaking into the sage on which she lay. He noticed she had picked up on the Sioux women's lilting singsong way of talking. She prayed in English, of course. "God in heaven, help me to survive this ordeal and find my dear husband. Lead my guide to Julian, wherever he is. People are falsely accusing Julian of things he didn't do. Help me and Mr. Fargo return Julian's honor for his sake and mine. And, please, God, have this over with fast. I'm burning up. Amen."

Fargo said. *"Metakuye oyasin,"* so the other woman would know she had finished.

Her prayer offered much thanks for the buffalo hunt during which nobody had been hurt.

Long Nose followed her. Like the warrior on Fargo's right, he prayed for strong enemies.

Running Bear also gave thanks for the successful hunt.

The medicine man prayed for a mild winter, then launched a song to start the third round without a break. At the conclusion of the three songs, the round ended. During the ensuing silence, Fargo heard the water in the geode being swished, then Swift Water gulp from the horn. Crazy Fire, contrary as ever, was giving a drink of water to each person. The cool horn came to Fargo. He drank some and poured the rest onto Melody. When the refilled horn came back to him, he nudged Melody on the shoulder and held the wet horn to her cheek. She propped on an elbow and gulped it dry. Fargo passed the empty horn to the other woman, who passed it on around to the medicine man for refilling.

After all had drunk, the fourth and final round began with a song, which was followed by after-prayers. Only Running Bear and Long Nose made brief prayers. Then they sang a song that thanked the spirits for coming to listen and sent them back to the spirit world.

At the conclusion Crazy Fire dumped the remaining water onto the stones. The mammoth jolt of excruciating, painful steam raised a chorus of closed-mouth screams. After another eternity, the fat man called for the flap to be pulled back.

A white cloud gushed out through the tiny opening. Crazy Fire, who had indeed turned around, squeezed outside first. All but Fargo and Melody quickly followed him.

The glow from the embers in the fire pit, a short distance from the opening, cast a measure of light inside the lodge, where Fargo still sat and Melody lay. He looked over his shoulder at her. If she wasn't dead, she might as well have been. The cool night air that displaced the heat didn't rouse her.

He dragged Melody facedown from the lodge, cradled her in his arms, and walked into the ice-cold pond. She came to life instantly, gasping, kicking, clawing, and screaming for him to get his hands off her. He dropped her, then surface-dived and swam underwater to emerge on the far side. He watched Melody thrash out of the water and stride most unladylike to her clothes. She plopped down on the ground and stared hard at him while she pulled on her boots.

He came out and went to his clothes piled near her. Dressing, he told her, "Melody, this sweat isn't over yet."

Her shoulders dropped, and she looked at him, her pleading expression clearly suggesting her total capitulation to an unknown but certain experience that would also prove horrible and uncivilized. She mumbled, "What now, Mr. Fargo? An orgy?"

He trapped a forming chuckle and answered, "No, ma'am. The white man hasn't yet taught the red savages that. We have to share the pipe, then we can go home to sleep."

"You take my place. I don't partake of tobacco. No proper lady would."

"Well, ma'am, it's time for you to get improper, because you are going to smoke the pipe."

"Oh? And what if I refuse?"

"Huh, you don't know what heat is. I'll steam you to near death, then hold you to the bottom of yon pond till you're near drowned. Don't fight it, Melody. You aren't expected to inhale the smoke. Take only one puff to send your prayer up into the universe in the smoke."

"One puff?"

"Just one and let it out. Your prayer, like all the others you heard in there, collected in the seven pinches of *cansase,*—tobacco, to you—in the bowl of the medicine man's pipe. The only way to send those prayers to the Great Spirit, God, is in the smoke, that which you exhale and that which wisps from the bowl. Don't forget to say, *'Me-tock-we-ahs-ee,'* after you finish."

"I heard that a lot of times. It means?"

"Literally, all of my relatives. Relatives include everything: earth, water, grass, birds, and all other creatures. Everything an Indian does has a purpose. Take that lodge door, for instance. They build the top of it so low that you are forced to get on your hands and knees to go inside. For that split moment you are made to remember your four-legged relatives. And so it goes with most everything else they have learned through generations of living as part of nature. Savages? I think not. The white man who led the attack on your husband's payroll wagon was a savage."

He stood and pulled her to her feet. Crazy Fire and the others had formed a loose circle between the fire pit and lodge to smoke the long-stem pipe held by the medicine man. Fargo and Melody wedged between Running Bear and Swift Water. Crazy Fire touched the burning end of a twig to the bowl and puffed till smoke appeared, then he passed the pipe to Swift Water on his left to start it moving around the circle.

Melody stared cross-eyed at the bowl two feet from her lips and sucked hard. Her jaws ballooned before she released the gush of smoke and muttered, *"Me-tock-we-ahs-ee."* She passed the pipe to Running Bear.

After all had shared the pipe and Crazy Fire took it apart, they drifted back to camp. The powwow was still in full swing. Fargo saw her to the door of Long Nose's tepee. Before she entered it, he told her to sleep well, that he'd see her in the morning. She pulled back and faced him, balled fists on hips, and snarled, "You big bastard, I hope you're satisfied."

"Satisfied?"

"Yes. Do you think I'm dumb? Mr. Fargo, I see through your little game."

"Game?"

"Yes, game! You're using these Indians' ways and customs to exact your will over me. You've lied to me, placed me in a position where I'd have no choice but to stand in blood and guts under a blazing sun, forced me to show my naked body to savages—and I suspect you took your pleasure feeling it while I was unconscious, made me suffer, nearly drowned me, made me fill my mouth with that stinking tobacco, and now, to top it all off, you tell me to sleep well in a goddamn tepee with a horrible man and four other women. Really, Mr. Fargo, you are more than a bastard. You're a first-class son of a bitch."

"One and the same, honey." He tipped his hat and walked away.

Running Bear's and Happy Flower's entwined bodies formed an elongated hump in the buffalo robes covering them. They lay still, sound asleep, breathing slow and even. The small fire burned brightly, its flickering flames casting dancing shadow-patterns on the inner surfaces of the conical tepee. Dancing Cloud lay beneath robes on the opposite side of the tepee. She'd unbraided her hair. It splayed outward on the robe. Her dark eyes watched his every move. Fargo started undressing.

He said, "Tonight I heard prayers to make the Crow and Shoshoni strong. Are they at war with you? I didn't think the Shoshoni hunted this far east."

"The Crow like Lakota women. They come to steal us and ponies. We fight. It isn't often we see Shoshoni. *Blokehan*—oh, it was so hot that day—many Shoshoni came through our hunting grounds. They were going to their hunting grounds, and had a white man's wagon and a big gun that goes boom. Long Nose saw them and told us. He wanted to fight them, but Swift Water said to let them pass."

"Were any white men with the Shoshoni?"

"I don't think so. Long Nose didn't say."

Fargo slipped his underdrawers down to his knees, stepped out of the garment and to the robes.

Dancing Cloud pulled the robes back and sat to touch her lips to his manliness. He favored her by reclining slowly so the eager lips could follow him down. She straddled his chest and bent to suck, her long hair cascading onto his thighs. He felt her lips tighten and draw the foreskin back, then her tongue begin circling the sensitive blood-swelling head. When she bore down to take in more, he took her by the thighs and pulled her black bush to his lips. Parting her tight, slender crevice with his thumbs, his tongue probed into the opening and swished around the tender-soft membrane.

She moaned and her breathing became hot and rapid.

As she squirmed in her obvious delight, he felt her body start to tremble. She came off it gasping for air and murmured, "So big, white man . . . *lee-lah wash-tay.*"

He reached up and cupped both of the small breasts and teased the nipples to stand erect and hard. She placed her hands over his and encouraged him to squeeze tightly and pull on them. Her back arched when he did. She looked over her shoulder and smiled at him, moaning, "I will bite my tongue and not scream like Happy Flower." She folded forward, grasped and massaged his scrotum with one hand, and returned his throbbing staff to her mouth with the other.

Fargo kissed the inside of her smooth thighs and on the slim, hard cheeks. She whimpered around his slickened hardness, "Take me, take me now. Make me happier."

He pulled her head back and shoved her to straddle down his flat, hard belly until her moist slit met his member. Her hips rose and his crown slipped inside the hotness. He felt her hands grasp his knees and her hair brush his legs as she bent and squatted to help make deep penetration. He went deep into the hot recess. She groaned, "Oh! Oh! It is . . . oh . . . tearing me . . . apart. But don't stop, please don't."

She squirmed her hips to force a pleasurable mating and, achieving it, squatted even further to maximize the thrill. Fargo set his hips to swaying to juice and dilate the nook. She responded by bouncing on the spiraling hard member, and squealed through clenched teeth, "Eeeeeyyaaayah, yiii yo . . . that is so good. More, big white man. Make it go deeper . . . and faster."

He pulled her back onto him and rolled her under him. She stared at him and trembled. He took an entire breast into his mouth. Her sweaty body writhed under his. Her fingernails raked his thighs, and she love-bit his ears. When he slid to the other breast and rolled the hard nipple between his teeth, she gasped, "I'm going to explode. Take me, take me . . . now! Ride me, *wasicun*, break me, please."

Her slender legs parted wide to fully open the begging sheath of joy and captured the hardness. He thrust. Her knees came up and clamped against his waist. They gyrated in opposing directions, each adding other movements at the same time to heighten their own pleasure, and in perfect cadence with the throaty drumbeat. Both breathed hard and moaned deliriously, her soft murmurs whispering, "I will not be the same again. Oh, this is so beautiful . . . so filling. I want it to last forever . . . eeeeeyaaaiii! What is happening?"

He felt her fingernails dig into his ass and she bit hard on his left pectoral muscle. The fierce contraction squeezing hard as blazes on his blood-swollen member had to be her first, he thought. When the contraction relaxed to grip anew, she screamed again, "Aaaaayyee-eeiii," and dug her heels into his buttock cheeks. "What is that down in me?" she cried. "I'm dizzy. I can't hear."

Her gigantic orgasm was followed by a series of lesser ones that triggered his eruption, which came on the abrupt halt of the drumbeat. With the first hot spurt, Dancing Cloud whimpered, "That's hot. Oh, it's hot. I'm on fire in there."

He slackened his pace somewhat. Her long legs dropped onto the robe. She lay panting with her legs and arms extended outward. He pushed up and their eyes met. Both smiled.

Fargo awoke at first light of the new dawn. Dancing Cloud's head was nestled in the crook of his right shoulder, her pretty face a picture of newfound bliss. Running Bear sat fully dressed on the other side of the fire he'd made to warm two pieces of meat on the sticks he held. Their eyes met and both men smiled.

In a low tone, Running Bear said, "We will eat first. Swift Water wants to council with you." He handed one of the meat-bearing sticks to Fargo.

Fargo eased the young woman's head onto the robe. Coming to a sitting position, he asked, "Do you know what it is about?"

The warrior's head shook. "Did Dancing Cloud make you happy? Her screams opened my eyes two times. Happy Flower said you will have to stay in another tepee next time."

They shared grins, devoured the juice-filled meal, then Fargo dressed, and they left.

Swift Water sat next to the glowing bed of embers left by the powwow fire. He was gnawing meat from what looked like a buffalo rib. When he saw the two men coming toward him, he flipped the bone over his shoulder. It landed between two prone dogs. They looked at it, then went back to sleep. Running Bear sat on Swift Water's right, Fargo on his left.

After a long moment of silence, the old man said, "Warriors say ten *wasicun* are near camp. They are not together. There are two groups of three. The other four are scattered. All arrived shortly after you and the woman. My warriors say they stopped and watched your woman from long distances, as though they didn't want her to know. They are strange people, Fargo. None wanted the others to see them. They followed our hunting party at great distances when it returned. I told my warriors to leave them alone, that I would talk with you about them. Do you want my warriors to kill them, Trailsman?"

"No, Grandfather. I saw them too. They have been following us since we left Fort Hope. They are greedy people, Grandfather. They are my problem, not yours. Their greed will kill them, if the Crow or Shoshoni do not."

The old man grunted for Running Bear to bring Long Nose to him. Swift Water and Fargo remained silent until the two warriors were seated. Swift Water asked Long Nose, "Our tall friend is going into Shoshoni lands. Tell him what you saw at the place of many bones last summer."

Long Nose cleared his throat and began, "I counted twenty Shoshoni warriors taking a wagon toward their hunting grounds. They had a long gun like the blue coats shoot tied to the back of the wagon. All of the warriors had rifles and firewater."

Swift Water hastened to add, "When Long Nose came back and told me this, I decided to let the Shoshoni pass without harm. I wanted you to know they have rifles and a long gun."

Fargo looked at Long Nose. "Were there any *wasicun* with the Shoshoni?"

Long Nose shook his head, then said, "No. A *wasicun* rode one moon in front of them. Another came one moon behind."

"Were either wounded?" Fargo probed.

"No."

"Was either a soldier, a bluecoat?"

"Yes. The man who followed wore a blue coat."

"And they—I mean, the two men—were riding in the same direction, the same as the Shoshoni?"

Long Nose nodded and puckered toward the northwest. "That way. Toward where Maka Ina spurts water high."

Fargo had seen the mighty geyser many times. He wondered if that was where the wagon had been taken, if the geyser was the place where the crooks were to meet. Fargo looked at Long Nose and asked, "Did you see anything else?"

The old man answered, "That is all we know, Trailsman."

"Grandfather, I thank you and Long Nose for telling me these things. Now my woman and I must leave our Sans Arc brothers and sisters. You and your people have been kind to us. We thank you."

Swift Water grunted, signaling this council had ended and the warriors and Fargo were dismissed.

Crossing the arena, Fargo asked Long Nose to awaken Melody and tell her it was time to leave.

Inside Running Bear's tepee Fargo rummaged in his saddlebags and brought out gifts. He gave Happy Flower a lady's hand mirror he'd been carrying around for months. He presented Dancing Cloud with the pearl necklace he'd won in a poker game at Gable's Saloon back in Independence. Running Bear received a French hideout gun and a palmful of bullets for it.

Running Bear went with him to get the Ovaro and black stallion. After making both horses ready to ride, they walked them to Long Nose's tepee and called Melody out.

The woman emerged haltingly, as though every bone in her body might break any second. When Fargo relieved her of her saddlebags, she glowered at him. "I hate you," she whispered.

He answered out the corner of his mouth, "The earrings. Did you—"

"No," she snapped and cut him off. "I'm keeping them."

"No, you're not," he told her. He dug into his saddlebags and produced the silver man's ring he'd won off the same stupid poker player at Gable's. Passing the ring to Melody he hissed, "Woman, I want to see you smile when you give this to Long Nose, but don't look him in the eye."

She forced the smile, presented the gift, and muttered, "I hope you're satisfied, Mr. Fargo."

"Not quite, ma'am." He asked Running Bear to take them to the virgin girl's tepee.

At the tepee, Running Bear tapped on its covering, gave his name, and asked for Many Laughs to come outside. The door flap opened and she stepped out.

Fargo elbowed Melody and said, "Give her the earrings."

"No. They cost five dollars. The little heathen would lose them."

"You take off those earrings and hand them to her." His hard stare preempted any rebuttal.

Grim-jawed Melody obeyed him.

The girl smiled, said, *"Pilamaya,"* and backed in through the opening.

Melody asked what *pilamaya* meant. Fargo told her, "Thank you. Many Laughs will cherish your gift for the rest of her life. She will tell her children and grandchildren about the white woman who gave them to her, and how she carried the fifty-six stones for her to sweat by. You have made a friend. In so doing, you have made a friend for other white women who come this way. Now, mount up and let's be on our way."

Riding out, they entered the clearing where Swift Water sat watching the morning sky change colors. Fargo reined to a halt and dismounted. He fetched a calabash pipe and a pouch of tobacco from the saddlebags and gave them to the old man. Swift Water smiled many wrinkles and said, *"Wash-tay, lee-lah wash-tay. Pee-lahm-ah-ya*, Trailsman. Have a safe journey and return soon."

Fargo nodded, eased up into the saddle, and nudged the Ovaro to a walk.

They'd gone less than a mile from the camp when he spotted one of the groups of three tracking them, riding parallel at a safe distance.

6

He waved for Melody to move up and ride alongside him. When she was there, he said, "Get rid of that grouchy face, Melody, and let's talk."

"To hell with you. I don't feel like talking to you. As a matter of fact, I hurt all over and didn't get a moment's sleep. I'm tired and mad."

"Then turn around and go back to Fort Hope." He dug in his pocket for the money she'd given him.

His suggestion jolted her. It showed in her tone of voice when she replied, "No, I can't do that. Put the money back, Mr. Fargo. Be patient with me, please. I'm not accustomed to your way of life. Give me a few days, and I promise I'll adjust; things will be different. You'll see."

What she said, the way she said it, made sense. He asked why she didn't sleep. "Was it because of the sweat?"

"No. While I'd never been that hot or miserable before, I have to admit it left me more relaxed than one might imagine. I was ready for a good night's sleep and would have gotten it but for . . . Well, how do I say it without sounding so vulgar?"

"Long Nose? Did he . . . ?"

"Fornicated all night. I—"

Fargo reined to a halt and stared at her.

Her head shook. "God, no, not with me, Mr. Fargo. With his two women, right there where I'd see and hear everything. They're animals, Mr. Fargo. No, worse than animals. Animals don't use their mouths. Oh, it was horrible. I buried myself under that stinking robe so I couldn't see them. I even put my fingers in my ears to shut out their sounds, but I could still hear them. It went on all night."

"I was told you really know how to skin and butcher buffalo. How's that? You didn't strike me as one who knew how."

"I grew up on my parents' ranch in Texas. That was before we moved to Kentucky and started raising Thoroughbreds. I'm an only child, Mr. Fargo. My father always wanted a son. He raised me as though I were one. I was skinning and butchering at an early age. That doesn't mean I enjoy it."

She had answered his question. He ventured into another subject. "You hired me to take you to Washington, but that's only part of it, isn't it? What is that other part?"

"I guess you're entitled to know. I have reason to believe Julian's alive and lost somewhere out here. I don't know; he may be hurt. There was a man—I never saw him—who approached Julian and suggested . . ."

Fargo waited for her to continue. When she didn't, he didn't mince words. "Look, Mrs. Abbott, I'm no fool. Your husband and another man conspired to steal that payroll. You know it, and so do I, so quit pussyfooting and tell me what you know."

"The man—and don't ask me his name because Julian never told me—Julian said the man told him it would be easy and nobody would get hurt. That, of course, was a lie.

"The plan was simple. The man was friendly with a large group of Shoshoni warriors who didn't like the way their chief was running things. They wanted guns to fight with.

"Anyhow, they would wait for the payroll wagon at this particular place and surprise everybody. It would be done and over in the blink of an eye. They would tie everybody, take the rifles and money, and go to Shoshoni country.

"The man would wait for Julian to join him at a certain place. Don't ask me where because I don't know. Julian said it was best that I didn't know. They would divide the payroll, then Julian would go to Seattle, from where he'd send word to me. I never heard from him."

"I guess you know that makes you a coconspirator and those troopers' blood is on your hands too?"

"Don't lecture me, Mr. Fargo. I love my husband. Nobody was supposed to get hurt."

Fargo wrestled with the decision he had to make. He could turn back and report the truth to the nearest army outpost, or continue northwest and search for the culprits. If he found one or both, he'd take them back to Ft. Laramie.

He opted for the latter, saying, "You were wise telling me this. Now I'll tell you what's going to happen. Your husband and the other man are alive, or at least I think they are. However, my sources say one of them is wounded. Both may still be holed up somewhere in the Wyoming Rockies. If they are, I'll find them. When I do, I'll kill them if I have to in order to get that payroll. Just wanted you to know, ma'am."

She sighed and said, "What's done can't be undone. Julian won't fight you, Mr. Fargo. I'll see that he doesn't. I don't care about the money. All I want is my husband back in my arms. We will make a new life for ourselves in Seattle."

Fargo wondered about that. He wondered about other things too. Like how big an idiot Julian Abbott really was to think his partner would actually go to the meeting place and wait there to divide the payroll with him. Thieves had no morals, certainly no integrity. Moreover, the lieutenant had no intention of contacting his wife. He'd gone along with the robbery plan to get rid of the domineering, bitchy woman.

Fargo said, "We should make it to the foothills of the Laramie Range by dusk. No fire tonight."

She didn't object.

They rode through a sea of waving grass that reached their mounts' knees. Their trackers rode on a semicircle behind them. All were barely visible. The two groups of three followed by at least a mile and were separated by about as much on the arc. Two riders rode point, one way out on Fargo's right, the other a similar distance on his left. The other two were spaced between the point riders and the groups. If Fargo could see them, he reasoned, each group had to know about the others.

Melody didn't seem to notice any of them. Tired and drowsy, she rode with her head lowered and her eyes closed.

All during the latter half of the sunny day he watched the Laramies appear on the horizon and loom larger and larger. As they came closer to the mountains, a cool breeze met them.

Melody looked into the red rim of sun lowering behind the range and asked, "How much farther, Mr. Fargo? I'm getting chilled and I desperately need to stop for a moment."

"We can stop here, but there are no bushes. Otherwise, you'll have to hold it a mite longer. There's a shady creek up ahead. That's where we'll stop and bed down for the night."

"Mr. Fargo, I will appreciate it if you watch your language. Just because we are alone and way out in God only knows where doesn't mean we have to abandon our good manners. I'll wait until we reach the stream. And, sir, I didn't like the way you said 'bed down.'"

"Oh? How did I say it?"

"Suggestive. I have no intention of sleeping with you, Mr. Fargo, so you can get that thought out of your mind. I'm a proper woman, sir, even out here."

Fargo chuckled. The first gust of cold wind, he thought, will blow your body straight to mine for warmth, and to hell with propriety. It had been his experience that proper women were the first to get mighty improper when it benefited them. He said, "Yes, ma'am, I won't utter another such implication."

They rode into the lengthening shadows to the shallow stream bordered with willows and conifers. He halted on the near bank, dismounted, and started unsaddling the Ovaro.

Melody hurried to find a bush.

He had both stallions stripped of their gear and hobbled for grazing when she returned. He spread their bedrolls side by side, separated by a saddle's width. Melody moved hers about twenty feet upstream and behind a low shrub. She came back and sat with him to eat beans and beef jerky.

Between bites, he said, "If it gets in there with you, remember to lie real still and hold your breath. Above all, don't scream."

"It? What, Mr. Fargo?" She cut her eyes left and right.

He finished eating before answering, "This place is crawling with them." He started digging a hole to bury the empty bean can.

"Them?" Much concern carried in her tone. "Mr. Fargo, do you mean snakes?"

He opened his bedroll and sat to pull off his boots. "Yes, ma'am, damn big ones. Sorry—that cuss word slipped out, ma'am."

She stood and eyed her bedroll. "I'm deathly afraid of snakes," he heard her confess softly.

"Funny thing about those whopper rattlers. They hear a person cuss, they won't come anywhere near him. You want to wash those tin plates for me?"

She squatted at the edge of the bank to wash them, but kept one eye on him and the other toward her bedding. Fargo took off his clothes and got into his sleeping bag. Melody left the plates on the bank and hurried to her bedroll. In the last light of day, he noticed, she got inside it fully dressed.

He lay awake for thirty minutes, then eased out of the bag and got dressed. He shaped the bedding to appear that he was asleep inside it, strapped on his gun belt, and forded the gurgling creek. On the far side he climbed up a pine and sat on a limb with his back against the trunk. There he waited for the moon to rise and somebody to come.

Fargo heard them before one presented himself obliquely. Three pair of boots crept slowly under the canopy hiding a deer path that followed the mountains' curvature on Fargo's side of the stream. The men were coming toward him. If in their wariness they weren't keenly alert, they would break out of their dark shield and pass over a short stretch of the pathway bathed in moonlight. Fargo swung his Colt around and leveled his aim heart-high on the black hole. All he needed to see was one boot tip.

They stopped short of the dark orifice, obviously to consider the clear area and select who would expose himself first. Through the night sounds Fargo heard them whispering. After a long moment of silence, they retreated several paces, then left the path and moved toward the rocky, spruce-infested rise on his right. Except for part of a jagged outcrop of brilliant red rocks that jutted into a sparse clearing, the area was consumed in near-total darkness. Within seconds he no longer heard them.

Listening, his gaze swept from the outcrop to his bedroll and back. A skilled rifleman could find an opening in the trees to shoot through. The bedroll did shine in the moonlight. Melody's lay hidden in darkness, not that it mattered; his saddle and Sharps beside his bedroll were more than enough to pinpoint him. He watched the outcrop.

After a few minutes the glint of a moonbeam kissed off metal in the rocks and, like a star exploding, caught his eye. The gleam vanished as quickly as it appeared, but Fargo had the spot fixed in his mind and sight. He aimed the Colt where the man's head should be, applied pressure on the trigger, then held it a hair's breadth away from releasing the hammer and waited for the rifles' muzzle flash.

The explosion from the Colt was absorbed in the rifle's retort. The combined sounds bounced off the rocky rise and echoed all along the creek. Melody screamed.

Fargo watched for movement in the outcrop and the

darkness behind and on both sides of it. Again the glint flashed, only this time it fell forward, and the rifle clattered on the rocks. Fargo waited.

Five seconds passed, then ten, before he heard a hoarse voice whisper far too loudly, "Cecil? You get the bastard, Cecil?" The concerned voice came from the left side of the rocks.

Fargo holstered the Colt and eased down the tree trunk. Moving left in a crouch, he flushed Cecil's confederates from where they hunkered behind a thicket. "No, Cecil missed the bastard." Then he gave them cause to worry. "You two are next."

Their presence revealed, they cast aside all caution and ran toward Fargo's left, headed downstream, quite obviously for their horses.

Fargo raced down the deer path to intercept them. Coming to the end of the foliage tunnel, he saw the three horses ground-reinded in an open area at the bank of the creek. He halted shy of breaking out of the canopy and waited. One behind the other, the men darted out from safety of the shadows and rushed toward their mounts. Fargo fired at the lead runner. The bullet knocked him down. The other man dived right, rolled onto his stomach, and fired blindly into the canopy opening. Slugs whizzed past Fargo's head.

"Get him, Duke," the wounded outlaw shouted. "Shoot the big son of a bitch!"

Fargo shot twice at Duke, snaking to safety in the shadows beyond the horses, and missed him by inches. He swung the Colt around to finish off the wounded man only to see he'd made it to the skittish horses.

Duke yelled, "I'm going after the woman. Hold him off, Lester, till I get her."

Fargo reloaded, waiting and watching for a clear shot at either man.

"No," Lester roared. "You stay here with me, goddammit. We'll get him first, then his whore."

"Like hell you will," Melody shouted. Her rifle barked two fast rounds into the soil near the horse's pawing hooves, where Lester stood crouched.

Duke fired twice into the tunnel, but Fargo had already moved. He circled around behind Duke to put the man between him and the moonlit bank where Lester and the horses stood. Fargo saw the silhouette of Duke's gun hand appear from behind the trunk of a large cottonwood, then his head came around to sight down the six-gun's barrel.

It was enough of a target for Fargo. He blew a hunk from Duke's skull. "You're next, Lester," Fargo pronounced calmly.

"No, Mr. Fargo," she cried. "He called me a whore. Let me kill the son of a bitch."

Lester was between them. Escape was impossible. He capitulated, tossed his revolver out into the creek for them to see and hear splash, and limped into view with his hands up. "All right," he said, "you got me cold. You can see I'm shot. Let's jaw."

Melody stepped out of the shadows on the far side of the stream and halted on the bank.

Fargo emerged from the trees and went to him. "You what's left of the men who tried to rob the bank?" Fargo asked.

"Yeah," Lester grunted. "Look, I'm hurt pretty bad an' bleeding fast. Why—"

Fargo interrupted him. "You three the ones who tried to gulch me in my hotel room?"

Lester hedged with a plea. "I ain't no threat to you no more, so why don't you lemme get on my horse an' try to make it back to Fort Hope?"

The rifle fired. Lester spun halfway around from the force of the bullet mushrooming through the left side of his back. He was dead before he hit the ground.

Fargo shook his head and looked at Melody. As she lowered the smoking rifle, he said, "Ma'am, I kept count. You said three vulgar words. Do you want to borrow my soap to wash out your mouth?"

"Fuck you," she spat.

He watched her wheel and stride toward their camp. Eyeing her swinging hips, he muttered, "In time, honey, in time." He removed the saddles and tack from the robbers' horses and set them free for Indians to find.

Back at the camp site, Fargo inspected the bullet hole in his bedroll. The hole was where his head should have been. "Damn good shot," he mused aloud.

Now that all the gunfire had those tracking them wide awake and on their toes, Fargo made a small fire and put a pot of coffee to brewing. Shortly Melody approached. She'd changed into a nightdress and had a dark shawl draped over her shoulders. She sat across the fire from him, drew her legs up, and rested her chin on her knees. Looking into the fire, she adjusted the shawl and said, "I couldn't go to sleep for smelling the coffee."

He poured two cups full and handed her one. "Where'd you learn to shoot like that?" he asked.

"In Texas. First jackrabbits, then coyotes. You're pretty good yourself. I nearly died when that first shot woke me up. I ran to see if you were all right. When I saw what I thought was you in that bedroll, lying so still and all . . . Well, then I heard your voice across the creek. That's when I got my rifle."

"To shoot me?"

"No. Are you crazy? Why would I do that?"

"I don't know. But it seems like a lot of people want me dead."

She sipped her coffee. "So I've noticed, Mr. Fargo. Trouble seems to follow you like a shadow." She stood, went to the creek, and rinsed out the cup. Handing it to him, she said, "I'm going to bed now. I'm rather tired. I'll see you at sunrise, Mr. Fargo."

He nodded and watched her walk into the shadows. He drank another cup of coffee, then undressed and got into his bedroll. He went to sleep listening to the night sounds.

Fargo's eyes snapped open at dawn. He glanced at the two hobbled stallions. They hadn't awakened him. He looked up and down the creek. Nothing was amiss. Melody, he thought. He got up and dressed, then went and peered over the brush that hid her.

She was in the bedroll, on her back, with only her head showing. She was wide awake, staring straight up, and sweat was rolling off her face. Her tense expression conveyed she was very frightened, and it appeared she was holding her breath.

Fargo stepped around the brush and went to her. She looked at him and tried to speak, but no words came through the trembling lips. He asked, "Ma'am, are you sick?"

She gulped and batted her eyes.

He knelt next to the bedroll and bent his ear to her mouth. He barely heard her say, "Snake."

He leaned back. "In there with you?" Her eyes batted furiously. "Don't move a muscle," he warned, "and don't be afraid. I'll get it out. I need to know where it is before I go feeling around in there. If it's on your left, bat that eye."

She batted both eyes.

"Hmnnn," he mused. "It's on you. Bat one eye for high, both for low."

Again he saw both eyes bat.

"Okay, one eye for a little snake, both for a whopper."

Her eyes fairly fluttered.

"Big one, huh? Well, you be real still and we'll see if we can get it without either of us getting bit. That'll be my hand you feel."

He slipped his right hand inside the bedroll, moved it down between her breasts, over her belly real slow, then slid his middle finger over her Venus' mound, and found the snake coiled between her thighs. The snake was indeed large. It had a fat body that rippled under his soft touch. He listened for the telltale buzz of rattles while moving his hand along the snake's body to find where it became skinny just below the head. When he came to where it slimmed, he said, "Honey, this is the moment of truth. Listen carefully. I'm going to grab this rascal behind the head. You'll know it when I do because that snake will raise hell.

When it does, you fling the bedroll open and get the hell out of there. Get ready."

He grasped behind the head. The snake jerked furiously and thrashed its body and tail under the covers. Melody threw the flap back and scrambled out. Fargo added his other hand behind the snake's head, pulled it out, and held it at arm's length. The body instantly coiled around his left arm and the biggest set of rattles he'd ever seen started buzzing. The snake's mouth was wide open, its fangs extended. Fargo didn't dare remove a hand from the angry snake, and he knew he couldn't hang on forever.

He said, "Reach inside my left pant leg and get my throwing knife. Slice its head off behind my hands."

She muttered, "I'm afraid."

He squinted at her and hissed, "You'll do it or I'll pitch this snake on you. Now move, dammit!"

She kept her stare on the snake's big head while fumbling for the knife. As she put it behind his hands, she gulped, closed her eyes, then sliced. The severed body came off Fargo's arm and wriggled onto Melody's foot, then coiled around her calf. She screamed and fainted. Fargo flung the head across the creek.

He carried her to his bedroll and tucked her inside it. She came around while he was making a fire for coffee. He said, "You did good. How do you feel?"

She took a deep relaxing breath before she answered, "Exhausted. Mr. Fargo, I'll be indebted to you forever. I was never so scared in all my life. I'm not cut out for this kind of life. I know now I should have never done this."

He set the coffeepot on the edge of the fire. After a few seconds he said, "It happens, ma'am. How long was it in there?"

"Forever. I owe you an apology."

"For what?"

"At first, I, uh, well, I thought—"

His head snapped around sharply and he cut her off. "You thought that was me? Honey, I don't sneak up on sleeping females."

"I said I apologize. Did you have to feel all over my, er, privates like that? Your hands are rough."

He chuckled. "Next time I'll leave you to figure out how to get it out." He poured her a cup of coffee.

After taking a sip, Melody said, "Mr. Fargo, I would appreciate it if in the future you didn't call me honey. I'm not your honey."

That woman never gives up, he thought, and shook his head.

7

Fargo rode west-northwest, through sweeping valleys and majestic canyons, over windblown ridges, and among the mountains in the Laramie Range. Everywhere he and Melody looked, nature was in the process of taking out her winter shawl. Many of the slopes they saw were now barren. He described to her how, in summer, they were covered with brightly tinted buttercups, dwarfed genitans, goldenrod, alpine forget-me-not, lupine, and saxifrage. Total bleakness did not now prevail, however. Crowded in the dense underbrush in quaking aspen thickets were mountain yellow rose, beaked hazelnut, and antelope brush. The golden aspen groves speared up mountainsides covered with yellow pine and Englemann spruce.

Pronghorn bucks herded their harems in sheltered hill valleys. There they would join others to migrate for the winter. The forests and lowlands, mountains and valleys fairly teemed with nature's creatures large and small. Fargo and Melody had plenty of fresh food.

Shortly before dusk four days after her encounter with the huge rattlesnake, they reached the east bank of the Sweetwater River. While Fargo hunted for supper, she made the fire and brewed coffee. She heard the Sharps be fired once. Five minutes later Fargo came back carrying a plump buff cottontail. He squatted on the bank to skin and clean it for roasting.

Melody said, "Mr. Fargo, my curiosity and your silence about the same thing has gotten the better of me. For several days I've heard rifles fire late in the day. Somebody else is obviously hunting. Who, Mr. Fargo? Indians?"

"Could be, ma'am. I haven't seen them either."

"You're not concerned?"

"No, ma'am. Not as long as they leave us alone."

She didn't press him any further. He left the rabbit in the shallow by the bank and stepped to a redbud that grew among low-growing ash trees. He cut two small limbs having forked branches, and one long straight section. She watched him shove the two forked pieces into the ground on either side of the fire, then peel the bark off the long piece. He asked, "What say you open a can of beans to go with this meat?"

While she did, he skewered the carcass on the long stick and set it in the forks. They sat on their bedrolls and stared into the fire, drinking coffee, waiting for the meal to cook.

"Mr. Fargo, would you mind if we rested here tomorrow? I'm tired. Could we stay out of the saddle for one day, to walk and just loaf in the sun for a while. Would that be all right with you?"

"Why, sure, ma'am. I'm in no hurry."

"Thank you." She stood with her back to the fire and faced north. After a moment she asked, "Is November always this warm? I expected cold, at least cool enough for a wrap after sundown."

"It's a Chinook, ma'am. They can happen when you least expect, and usually when you need them most. They go away about as fast as they come up. Who knows, tomorrow it could be freezing."

She turned abruptly to face him. "Are you serious, Mr. Fargo? I did hear you say freezing?"

"Yes, ma'am. The first snow often flies in November. We'll see plenty of it before we see Seattle. I think the rabbit is done."

Halfway through the meal she announced, "I believe I'll take advantage of the warm weather and bathe."

"Ma'am, that water's mighty cold, but upstream a stone's throw there's a wide spot with good-sized boulders on either side. It's deep enough for you to sit on the bottom with your head out."

She nodded and said, "I'll take your word for it."

After she left, carrying a towel and her rifle, Fargo washed the cooking utensils and plates, then went downstream to bathe also. As he submerged to get the shock over with quickly, a bullet churned the water by his head so close he almost missed hearing Melody scream. He dived and swam underwater to the far side and eased his head up among trunks of fallen diamond willow to look about.

He heard somebody walking slowly through the tall wheat grass behind him. He sank down and waited. When he came up to take a look, he saw the dark form of Calvin Boggs standing on the bank less than five yards from him. Rick's quiet cousin held a revolver and scanned the stream.

Rick's voice broke the silence. "You okay, Cal?"

"Yeah," Cal answered. "I think I got him. Nobody can stay down that long. What about her?"

"She's gotta come up for air sooner or later. Come on down here and help us catch her when she comes out. Whoever catches her gets the first piece." Rick laughed and said, "Hear that, sweetie? There's only three of us and we don't mind sharing. So come on out and get it over with."

Fargo watched Cal step back and move upstream. When he left, Fargo swam underwater to the other side and got his Colt and Arkansas toothpick. He ran crouched through the thickets to come even with the boulders. The three men were about ten yards from him. Rick stood on tall flat rocks on the near side of stream and Leon stood on a smooth boulder across the pool from him. Cal waited and watched from the far bank below Leon.

Fargo leveled the Colt at Rick's back and applied pressure on the trigger. Rick dived into the water just as the Colt's hammer fell. Melody's piercing scream punctured the roar from the Colt. Leon apparently saw the muzzle flash, for he shot twice, both slugs missing Fargo by inches. Fargo was forced to retreat into the thickets. Leon's next bullets followed him all the way.

Fargo listened to a struggle going on in the water while he moved to another position downstream. Melody Abbott was fighting for her life, screaming and cursing at Rick. Cal yelled above Melody's screams, "Let her go, Rick! We might get him and her, but he might get one of us. We'll take 'em another time."

Fargo dived from cover onto the bank. Cal spotted him and leapt for safety behind the boulders before Fargo could fire. Leon had disappeared too. Rick jumped onto the bank and rolled to safety behind rocks. Fargo shot twice to intimidate them, then sprinted up the bank to the big stones across from them.

"Melody, are you all right?" Fargo shouted. "Can you see the bastards?"

"No," she hollered. "I think they ran away."

He heard horse's hooves pounding off downstream. He eased around the boulder and into the water. "Where are you?" he asked.

"Over here." Her voice came from the far boulders.

"Well, they're gone, for the time being. You can come out now. We can't stay here tonight, so I suggest you hurry."

She swam toward him, saying, "My towel's with my clothes on the bank. Would you please get it for me. I'm about to freeze to death. This is the worst mistake of my life."

He held the towel open for her when she staggered out of the stream. She pulled it around her, fell against his chest, and started sobbing. He held her trembling body close. She murmured, "Why, Mr. Fargo, why? Why do these horrible men want to kill you? Why have they followed us? Why, Mr. Fargo, why?"

"Uh, well, ma'am, I do think they want your body." He wanted to add, "And your knowledge," but held it back.

She spun away from his embrace. Glowering at him, she spat, "That's all you men think about—forcing yourselves on helpless females. Please turn around while I get dressed."

"I'll do better than that. I'll see you back at camp." He turned and walked away.

"Wait," she called out. "What if they come back."

He answered over his shoulder, "Honey, you can't have it both ways. Either take me as I am, or them as they are. Your choice." He kept walking.

Melody was tying her bedroll when he came back from dressing downstream. He noticed she'd also doused the fire and tied up his bedroll. Clearly, Melody Abbott was ready to get the hell out of there. Within minutes their saddles and gear were on the stallions. They rode at a gallop upstream until Fargo reckoned it was safe to slow to a walk.

He watched the Big Dipper move around the North Star. When it hung in the midnight position, he started looking for a place to bed down. He found it in the foothills of the Big Horns, a cave large enough to accommodate them and the horses.

Inside, he struck several matches so they could orient themselves with their surroundings. He led the stallions to the back wall, where he looped their reins around man-sized rocks, then went outside and gathered an armload of blue grass for the horses. Melody spread their bedrolls side by side and got into hers. He undressed a second time this night and crawled into his bedding.

She spoke softly. "Mr. Fargo, I do appreciate you. Not once have you made an advance on me. And God knows you could have any number of times. I must confess I expected you would. I want you to know that I was prepared to shoot you the first chance I got after you did. I no longer have to feel concerned because I know now you are a good and decent man. Having said that, would you like to kiss me good night?"

He rolled away from her and replied, "No, ma'am, I've already kissed my pinto."

"Men," he heard her mumble.

*   *   *

The Ovaro's low knicker snapped Fargo's eyes open. Dawn's first light illuminated the mouth of the cave and the dozen or so armed warriors hunkered inside it.

Fargo stared into the barrels aimed at him and said, "Wake up, Melody, but don't speak or look them in the eye."

8

Fargo knew from the headbands worn by two that they were Crow. The six eagle feathers in other warriors' hair meant they'd taken as many scalps. War paint left no doubt they were not hunting for breakfast. Their stolid gazes warned him not to make any sudden moves. He drew his hands from inside the bedroll slowly, so they could see he was not armed. He spoke and understood enough of their dialect to get by. "Good morning, my Crow brothers."

Melody, buried from sight in her bedroll, muttered, "Please, Mr. Fargo, be quiet and let me sleep. Mornings aren't my best hours. You know that. Wake me when the coffee's ready."

"Oh, it's ready, ma'am. I recommend you stay buried till I learn what these Crow warriors have on their minds for us."

He saw her bedroll jerk. "Crow?" she gulped.

"Yes, fourteen of them. I'm looking at as many scalping knives. I hasten to add that the Crow favor strawberry-blond hair over all others. I hope you have some clothes on."

He heard her groan and say, "Mr. Fargo, please don't play games with me. You're frightening me with talk like that. Tell me you're joking."

One of the Indians—a husky young man with a broad nose and wearing a bone choker and sporting two eagle feathers—broke a grin and in English said, "He's not joking, woman."

In a stronger voice she cried, "Oh, my God!"

"Yeah, well, dressed or not, I think you better come out of there." He looked at the English-speaking

95

warrior and said, "My last name is Fargo. Some call me the Trailsman. Tell the others I am their blood brother. We come in peace."

Melody poked her head out far enough to see the warrior when he said, "I am Long Bow, son of Chief Fights Plenty. Are you the white man who smoked the pipe with him many summers ago?"

"Yes, Long Bow, I am. Will you take us to your father?"

"That is not for me to say, Trailsman. Our leader, Has No Pony, will say." He glanced at Melody. "It does not offend me for you to look into my eyes, but you should not look into those of my brothers." When she glanced away sharply, he stood and went outside.

Fargo eased the bedroll back and dressed under the watchful eyes of the Crow warriors. To his surprise, Melody was stark-naked and made no attempt to hide her body when she came out of the bedroll. He said, "Are you crazy? Get back in there and put on some clothes."

Putting on her shirt, she commented, "I'm at my wits' end, Mr. Fargo. I simply don't care anymore about what will or will not happen to me. I've resigned myself to the fact I'm in a place where I don't belong and they can do with me what they will any time they choose. If I'm to end up having a Crow's babies, then it's my fault, not yours. I forced myself on you." She slipped into her underwear, then sat to pull on her Levi's and boots.

Long Bow entered the cave with a stocky, bull-necked warrior several years older than he. The man wore a bonnet adorned with at least a dozen eagle feathers. Long Bow introduced him as Has No Pony, adding rather solemnly, "You can live, Trailsman, but he wants the woman's scalp to hang on his tepee pole."

Fargo stepped between Melody and Has No Pony. "Tell him that he will have to kill me first and that I won't die easy or fast. Tell him I challenge him in a fight of his choice. Tell him if he is brave and not a coward who takes women's scalps he will fight me. Tell him those words, Long Bow."

Fargo listened to Long Bow translate his scalding dare to Has No Pony. Of course all of the other warriors heard it too. Fargo had presented Has No Pony with a classic face-saving problem. Has No Pony could murder both of them and take their scalps, or fight Fargo. If he did the former, it would be a shallow victory, one that wouldn't be talked about around council fires. Fargo knew the Indians liked to brag about how hard they had to fight to claim a scalp. The more vicious the fight, the more meaningful the brag. Has No Pony would accept the challenge.

And he did, in a most offhanded way. Expressionless, he shrugged, muttered, "Bring them along," and strolled outside as though there were no question in his mind about the eventual outcome.

He's a cocksure bastard, Fargo thought. He told Melody, "Relax, honey. I just saved your pretty ass."

"Mr. Fargo! Watch your language! Because we're in a bad predicament it doesn't mean we have to—"

"Oh, shut up, Melody, or I'll turn them loose on you here and now."

"You wouldn't."

"He would, madam." Long Bow chortled.

"What next?" Fargo asked Long Bow.

"Saddle your horses. Has No Pony will say outside. Any whiskey in those saddlebags?"

"Not one drop," Fargo replied. "Where did you learn how to speak English."

"Scouted for soldiers at Fort Laramie. My father said if we were to fight them, some of us should know their language."

They made the stallions ready for the trail and led them outside. Fargo counted twenty-six mounted braves. More than half held carbines. The others carried shields, bow and arrows, lances, and war clubs.

Six maidens waited for the order to start walking. They stood erect, proud and arrogant, and showed their defiance and disrespect for their captors by looking the men in the eyes. The fact all six had ugly bruises changed nothing; Indian women knew how to take beatings. It was expected in captivity. So young, thought Fargo, yet already hardened. Two were so young he reckoned this hunt might have been their first.

A lithe man wearing buckskin leggings held the war party's colorful staff. A dozen spotted eagle feathers were tied to its long shaft. Between the fluttering feathers hung freshly acquired scalps, all with long black hair.

Fargo wondered when, where, and how Has No Pony would take up the challenge. It didn't appear now and here was the time or place. He told Melody, "Mount up and follow me. This is not going to be your day of rest."

Has No Pony sent two of his braves to ride ahead and scout. They left at a gallop. When they were out of sight, the staff-bearer held the staff high and pointed the curved end due north. The party moved out at a walk. Long Bow rode alongside Fargo.

Fargo asked, "Where did you get the scalps? We haven't seen any of your red brothers in several days. Not even any signs."

"Snake people. They were in the west. A big hunting party. They had killed many buffalo. We attacked while they were skinning." Long Bow paused to grin and wink at Fargo, then explained, "A classic army pincer attack surprised them. Some got away, though. We chased them east until the night saved them from our bullets and arrows. We think they turned south after dark.

"Has No Pony made camp near where you did. We were far downstream of you. We heard gunfire. He sent two scouts. They found your fire and saw prints of two shod horses that galloped north. We knew it was white men. It was too dark to go after them. Has No Pony believed the white men were enemies, trying to kill each other. He said we would catch the survivor today. Who were you shooting at?"

"A cougar," Fargo lied. They had obviously missed spotting the trackers. Fargo's opinion of the eight went up. He wondered where they were and if they had the stuff it took to continue their pursuit into hostile Crow country. "After missing it, I decided it best to leave the area. Are we going to Fights Plenty's camp?"

"Yes. Four suns north."

Fargo mentally calculated the distance. "Near the Medicine Wheel?"

Surprised, Long Bow looked at him. "You have seen it?"

"Once."

"The camp is by the stream that flows south of the mountain."

Both the river and mountain revived old memories tucked in Fargo's mind, not necessarily fond ones. His first encounter with the Crow had occurred on the river. Four warriors wielding scalping knives leapt from atop the craggy boulders through which Fargo rode and pulled him out of the saddle.

Snorting its fright, the Ovaro reared and came down pawing. One of its deadly hooves crushed a warrior's skull. Fargo could still recall the bone-crunching sound.

Tumbling on the ground with the other three, one lost his knife and scrambled to retrieve it. Fargo kicked him in the jaw.

He seized the knife hands of the other two and twisted them violently until one's wrist snapped. The man screamed and fell back staring at his contorted and limp lower arm. With his free hand Fargo drew his throwing knife and sliced the other fellow's belly open.

The broken-jawed warrior staggered toward him, his knife poised to kill. Fargo threw the knife at the man. It buried hilt-deep slightly left of the warrior's breastbone.

By the time Fargo pulled the blade out and turned to put an end to the man with the shattered wrist, the warrior had fled to his pony and beat a hasty retreat.

Within the hour many Crow rode in from all directions and surrounded him. Escape was impossible. To fight them invited a certain death. He opted to surrender and take his chances. They bound him at the ankles with his own rope and tied it to his saddlehorn, then dragged him to their camp. There they threw him at the feet of Chief Fights Plenty and Iron Face, the medicine man.

Iron Face brandished a huge war club and moved to kill him on the spot. Fights Plenty's right hand shot out and grabbed the onrushing black stone in the nick of time to prevent it from bashing Fargo's skull.

The two men stood next to Fargo's battered and bleeding semiconscious body and argued at length. Fights Plenty won the heated debate, for not only was Fargo released, they returned his weapons.

That was not the end of it, however. After feeding him and watching while he tended to his scrapes and bruises, Chief Fights Plenty signed he was free to go. The old chief actually smiled. Fargo believed he saw admiration in the old man's clear eyes. They even shook hands before Fargo mounted up and rode east along the south bank.

Less than two miles away from the camp, he rounded a blind bend and came face to face with the angry medicine man and a dozen warriors with arrows aimed to kill. Under directions from Iron Face they stripped him naked, threw his garments and weapons on the bank, and hauled him out into shallow swiftly running icy water. They used his rope and their own to tie him spread-eagled faceup, and left him there to die slowly at the frigid hands of the water spirits.

The water's depth was such that as long as he remained conscious he could hold his mouth and nose out of it to breathe. He struggled on his bindings only to realize it was wasted effort; the water and his wrenchings secured the knots even tighter.

Numbness set in; his death was imminent. Sputtering, burning up his waning energy, he watched the sun go down behind the mountain. The pinto knickered lowly, as though clearing his throat.

Fargo took a final breath and closed his eyes to succumb to the inevitable. Water seeped through his lips and into his nostrils. The voice of the gurgling stream faded. His brain shut down.

He opened his eyes and saw a spiral of poles. Somebody grunted. He squinted toward the sound. Chief

Fights Plenty sat cross-legged on the other side of the small fire and stared at him. Fargo lay on his back, covered with warm buffalo robes.

He stayed in the chief's tepee for five days. During that time they came to communicate fairly well in sign language augmented with drawings in the soil ringing the fire pit. Fargo learned what had happened. The warrior whose guts he spilled was the medicine man's only son. That, at least, explained Iron Face's anger and desire for revenge.

Chief Fights Plenty intervened in his belief that any man, white or red, who could survive an attack by four Crow warriors was indeed worthy and deserved to live. He forbade Iron Face to kill him. The medicine man simply went about it another way, one that would serve the same purpose, and at the same time save his own hide from Fights Plenty's wrath. Hence the ordeal of water torture in the cold mountain stream.

When Iron Face and the warriors returned to camp, Fights Plenty noticed the buckskin aprons worn by several were darkened by water. He sent men both up and downstream. Fargo was found and brought back. After failing two times to kill the white man, Iron Face reluctantly agreed to leave him alone.

And he did, until the second encounter two years later. Fargo was passing through Crow territory, heading for Montana on a mission for a preacher whose young daughter had been captured by the Gros Ventre. He decided to visit his benefactor, Fights Plenty, to see if he knew anything about the girl.

Fights Plenty was away with a war party, headed west to collect the scalps of neighboring Shoshoni who encroached on Crow hunting grounds. These clashes over hunting rights were common and didn't last long. Fargo opted to wait for Fights Plenty to return.

Iron Face acted as though he'd resigned himself to his son's death. He greeted Fargo warmly, fed him, and offered him three young maidens to select from as bed partners. Fargo told him he would think on it. That night Iron Face came and asked if he'd ever seen the Medicine Wheel. Fargo signed no.

"Sometimes," Iron Face signed, "not always, presence at the sacred Medicine Wheel during the quiet of night provides one with a vision. I will take you there. Perhaps the spirits at the Medicine Wheel will appear and give you a vision of where to find the girl you seek."

Fargo agreed to go, not expecting to receive a vision, although one would be welcomed, but because he wanted to see the holy site Fights Plenty had told him about. According to the chief, the ancient Medicine Wheel was on top of the mountain when his Crow ancestors first arrived. In the absence of any firsthand knowledge, it was presumed the spirits had built it. This belief was supported by the many supernatural occurrences that happened on the mountain. Visions were but one such occurrence. So Fargo went up the mountain with his former enemy.

No sooner had they reached the summit than Fargo was overpowered by a dozen warriors who appeared out of nowhere. This was strange because he knew none had followed them, and there was no place on the relatively flat and barren site for that many warriors to hide. Again he suffered being stripped naked, this time to be tied spread-eagle on the rocky surface. When they muscled him to the ground but before being bound, he managed to insert a pebble into his mouth.

Iron Face stood over him and signed, "Remember your vision, white man. It will come as the sun spirits cook you. They will tell you its meaning when you cross over the Great River and enter the Spirit World."

Fargo lay facing the blistering sun for two days and shivering in the cold mountain air for three nights. His lips parched and burst. Huge blisters formed and broke, releasing juices that streamed over his body and aching limbs, drying and causing an itch that drove him to the point of insanity. The lifesaving pebble on which he sucked slid down his throat the evening of the third day. He was exhausted, too weak to fight the ropes any longer. His hearing screeched maddeningly, and it seemed as though his eyelids fluttered of their own accord. His brain couldn't assimilate these strange occurrences. His head lolled and he raved incoherently. Then all went black.

He awakened staring up at a spiral of poles. Two maidens, one on either side of him, were on their knees, washing his body with sopping wet beaver pelts. Fights Plenty watched their every move from beyond the fire. Seeing he was awake, one of the maidens dipped her pelt into a geode of water and offered it to him, indicating he should suck on it. He did eagerly, then gulped from the water supply in the geode.

Fights Plenty signed, "This is unfortunate, Trailsman. I have punished Iron Face for disobeying me. I cut off one of his arms. He will not bother you again. Neither will he ever disobey me again."

This time Fargo recuperated six days in the chief's tepee. Fights Plenty told him where to find the girl. On the seventh day he felt strong enough to ride. Before he left, he went to Iron Face's tepee and asked the one-arm man to interpret the screeching, fluttering vision he had before the black void came.

Iron Face signed, "You had no vision, white man. The vision will come the next time we meet. It will come on the fourth night of your ordeal with the spirits at the Medicine Wheel."

That had been four years ago. Since then Fargo had not seen the mountain or the stream that flowed on the south of it. Now it appeared that was about to change.

As he looked at the six captive Shoshoni females, striding barefoot over the rocky ground as though they could and would continue forever without a whimper, he found a new resolve and strength.

He knew he would need both. Iron Face still had one good arm and both legs.

9

At sunset on the fourth day, the column of warriors, with Has No Pony in the lead, trudged into Fights Plenty's camp. Women and children rushed to greet them, look at their captives, and the scalps adorning the staff, over which all made a big to-do. Has No Pony thrust his chest out and bragged continuously while he strutted about, relating how fierce the Shoshoni fought. Not once did he give any credit for the victory to his warriors.

Chief Fights Plenty emerged from his tepee and caught sight of Fargo instantly. As he came toward him, smiling, Fargo dismounted. They shook hands. Fights Plenty motioned for Long Bow to join them. Now that the old man had an English-speaking son, they communicated easily.

"Welcome, Trailsman. I see you now have a woman by your side. Tell her she can raise her eyes and speak to me."

Of course Melody heard the translation. She glanced up and smiled prettily. "Please tell him he's kind, and I appreciate it. Mr. Fargo, Long Bow, I am in desperate need of a toilet."

Fights Plenty wanted to know what she said. After Long Bow told him, the old man smiled. He shouted to one of the women, who came with eyes downcast. When Fargo saw her eyes flare, he knew she'd been told to escort the white woman down the stream. The woman grunted and gestured for Melody to follow her.

Long Bow said, "Father asks if you are well and

how long you can stay. He will have the women erect a tepee for you and your woman."

"Tell him I am fine and thank him for inquiring. We will leave as soon as possible, within two sunrises, unless your father wishes us to remain longer. Is Iron Face still around?"

Long Bow conveyed his comments, to which the chief replied, "Yes. It's amazing how obedient a one-armed man can be when reminded daily how fragile his good arm is. Father asks where you are going." Long Bow made a comment of his own. "I was on my first hunting party the first time you came, and scouting for the army the second. But I heard the stories about your troubles with our medicine man. Has No Pony is his nephew, the only one."

Fargo grimaced. "Tell him I am taking the woman to the great waters in the west. To—"

Long Bow's chuckle cut him short. "To where exactly, Fargo? Washington? California? Maybe Oregon? We know of those places. I have taught him to stop calling the Pacific Ocean the Great Waters."

"Seattle, Washington. She's looking for her husband, who vanished last summer after being attacked by Shoshoni."

"Shoshoni, huh?" He proceeded to translate.

Fights Plenty studied the ground, obviously in deep thought, before replying. Long Bow said, "Father wants to help you. He asks if you will stay to stand on the hill. Before you answer, Fargo, I warn you, Iron Face will direct the Vision Quest. Father believes, and I agree, the spirits will show you a vision of where to find the man attacked by our Snake enemies. What do I tell him?"

Fargo weighed the probabilities of the medicine man's actions against those of finding Melody's husband alive. While he didn't like the odds, he said, "Say I have given it thought and decided my Crow brother has much wisdom. I will be pleased and honored for Iron Face to stand me on the hill. You will be nearby, Long Bow? Just in case?"

"Nobody will be nearby," the warrior replied. He translated Fargo's decision to his father.

When the old man grunted and nodded, Fargo said, "You might mention my problem with Has No Pony."

"Oh, yes. I'd forgotten all about that." He and the chief talked at length. Fargo discerned a hint of concern in the old man's expression and voice. It was as though he wished he hadn't heard of the challenge. Finally, Long Bow said, "Father says there is nothing he can do but honor Has No Pony. Also, it is Has No Pony's decision as to when to carry out your challenge."

"And the how of it," Fargo reminded. "Personally, I would like to have it done and over before I go on the hill."

"I'm sure you would," Long Bow agreed. "After four days and nights on the hill without food or water, you'd be an easy kill for Has No Pony."

"Yes, and it gets worse. Iron Face would hang my scalp on his tallest tepee pole. Take me to Has No Pony."

Fights Plenty went with them. They learned Has No Pony had gone to see his uncle, the medicine man. Fights Plenty entered Iron Face's tepee without bothering to make the customary slap on the tepee covering. Neither did he say his name. Long Bow and Fargo followed him inside.

Iron Face and his nephew sat across the fire from each other. Both glanced up and leveled angry eyes on Fargo. The chief sat beside his medicine man. He gestured for his son and Fargo to sit by Has No Pony. Iron Face and Fights Plenty conversed in low tones. Fargo watched Iron Face's eyes dart from him to Has No Pony several times. At the conclusion of their conversation, Iron Face simply nodded and looked at Long Bow, clearly implying he could speak up.

Long Bow asked, "What do you want me to say to him, Fargo? In case you missed it, my father mentioned putting you on the hill. If I heard it, so did Has No Pony."

It made no difference to Fargo. He'd planned to

mention it himself at the outset. "Tell him I hold no grudges. Say I think he is a good and wise leader. In your own words tell him I don't want to fight him. At the end say I will if I must."

Long Bow spoke at length, after which Has No Pony made a brief comment. Long Bow sighed and reported, "He will fight you after you come down from the hill."

Fargo nodded and offered his hand to Has No Pony, who spat on it. Fights Plenty gasped, then admonished the warrior severely. Has No Pony glowered at Fargo throughout the dressing-down. When Fights Plenty finished, Has No Pony rose, nodded, and left in haste.

Outside, Long Bow told Fargo, "Father told him it was a bad mistake to spit on the hand offered in peace. He told Has No Pony he'd made an enemy and filled him with a great resolve, that he better choose his method and place for the challenge with much caution. He told him other things also, that it might be Has No Pony's scalp hanging on your saddle."

"I don't think it will go that far. The spirits willing, I'll beat him senseless and let it go at that. He is a good leader. I'd much prefer making friends with him."

They sat and watched two women finish erecting a tepee for Fargo and Melody. As the women were carrying sleeping robes inside, Melody and her escort arrived. Fargo stood.

"Our new home?" Melody asked.

Fargo nodded.

One of the women came out and went to a spit nearby. They watched her carve two hunks from a venison roast. She stabbed each piece with a sharp-pointed skewer fashioned from a thin limb and took them inside. A wisp of smoke curled out of the top opening of the tepee.

"Our supper," Fargo remarked.

"Smells delicious," she replied. "But it's those robes that have my attention. A few days ago nobody, not even you, Mr. Fargo, could have convinced me I would look forward to sleeping between buffalo robes. I'm tired of sleeping on the hard ground."

Fargo thought she was actually eager to get inside the tepee with him. He'd expected her to kick up a fuss, demand separate quarters. He wondered how far her sudden change in attitude went. He inquired, "After we eat, would you like to knock off the first layer of trail dust?"

She stiffened. "Mr. Fargo, are you suggesting—"

"No," he hurried to say. "I'm suggesting we're filthy."

She looked at him and smiled. "Yes, we are. A bath sounds wonderful."

Long Bow gave directions to a calm cove on the stream, then departed. Fargo followed Melody inside the tepee.

Half an hour later they were undressing on the bank of the moonlit cove. He asked, "Ma'am, why is it you no longer hesitate to undress with me looking on?"

"Don't get your hopes up, Mr. Fargo. I have absolutely no desire to bed with you. My nudity is, in certain instances such as now, a matter of expediency. I'd rather be naked in the water with you than caught alone in it by Crow men."

"I see," he said, and dived in.

True to her word she gave no direct encouragement for him to take her. Neither did she divide the cove and order him to stay on his side. She had a way of surface-diving extremely slowly. The movement was as graceful as her rump when it rolled up into view, glistened briefly in the moonlight, then submerged with hardly a ripple. When she executed it with her back to him, for an instant he caught a glimpse of her lower charm and became aroused. He wondered if she teased on purpose or without conscious thought.

Occasionally she stood in the waist-deep water, tilted her head back, and wrung water from her hair. During the movements her breasts came up and stuck out round and supple, the tiny nipples things of beauty. Bitchy though she was, Melody Abbott was nevertheless lovely and excitingly shapely of body.

They dressed and returned to the tepee. While Fargo rekindled the fire and added wood to knock off the night chill, she sat and undressed for bed.

"When do we leave?" she asked. "I presume we can go?"

He answered while he undressed. "Not for a few days. In the morning I begin a four-day Vision Quest. After that I have to fight Has No Pony. If I survive both, then we can leave."

"Vision Quest? I don't understand what you mean."

"It's a long story, one that wouldn't interest you. Essentially, I hope to see if your husband's alive or dead and where to find him or his body."

"Mr. Fargo, Julian is not dead. My husband may be weak-minded, but he is strong of body. But you are right: I'm not interested in your flair for doing Indian things. God erred when he failed to make an Indian out of you. Will the two of you brawl, fistfight? While you're at it, why on earth do you men always want to beat on each other? You seem to relish fighting."

"It isn't so much a case of want-to as a case of have-to. It's the times and the place. I didn't make the rules."

She rolled onto her left side, putting her back to him. When she drew her knees up, the top robe pulled away and exposed her bare fanny. She muttered, "Maybe not, but you damn sure seem to enjoy them. Good night, Mr. Fargo. Keep your hands to yourself."

Sleep evaded him for a while, until she moved slightly and the robe on top slipped down and covered her fine ass and the exciting bushy vee the shadows of the flickering flames seemed to set in motion.

A slapping on the outside of the tepee awakened him. Long Bow said, "Reveille in there. It is time."

"Be with you in a minute," he called back. He looked at Melody. She was facedown, breathing slow and easy, completely oblivious that she was engulfed by warm robes in a tepee erected by savage Indians. He dressed and went outside.

The first stage of dawn revealed a clear sky, with air

109

chilly enough to raise gooseflesh. All was quiet. Long
Bow led the way to the sweat lodge. Two half-naked
warriors squatted near the fire heating the stones within.
Iron Face and his nephew sat with their backs against
the curvature of the lodge. They stood when Fargo
and Long Bow walked in. Iron Face spoke briefly to
Long Bow.

"He wants to know if you've ever done this," Long
Bow reported dryly.

"No. I have, however, heard about it several times."

Long Bow translated to the medicine man, who
grunted his response, which the young warrior translated. "He said that because you are white, you're
weak and might die. Iron Face doesn't want to lose his
other arm. While there will be no food for you, he is
going to leave water for you to drink. Other than that,
things will proceed more or less as you know them. I
say more or less because each medicine man's spirits
guide him differently. But in the end it's the same—
four days and nights alone, praying, crying for a vision
from the spirits."

Fargo nodded and said, "Tell him to forget the
drinking water."

Iron Face smiled when he heard Fargo's response.
He stepped out of his moccasins and disrobed. Fargo
did likewise, then crawled inside the lodge and sat in
the west, the honor position on the circle. Long Bow,
then Has No Pony entered next and sat in the south.
Iron Face crawled in and sat at the north of the opening. A geode filled with water was handed in. Iron
Face handed Fargo a buffalo horn and allowed him to
drink his fill, his last water until he came off the hill,
or until he died, whichever came first. He drank four
hornsful.

They remained silent while Iron Face ceremoniously
filled the bowl of a long-stemmed pipe with sacred
tobacco and capped it with a ball of sage. The pipe
moved from Has No Pony to Long Bow, who passed it
to Fargo. He knew to grasp the bowl in both hands

and tilt the stem out, a position he would maintain throughout the Vision Quest, beginning here and now.

Seven stones came in, all the size of small watermelons, all white-hot. The flap came down. Iron Face and the two warriors started singing, calling in the spirits. The stones sparkled briefly. What appeared to be fireflies flitted about the interior momentarily, then collected above the stones and fell to disappear in them.

Throughout the several songs they sang, Iron Face poured water on the stones. As he sweated profusely, Fargo willed his body to relax. The lengthy round finally ended. The flap came up. Steam boiled out through the scant opening. Through it Iron Face smiled at Fargo, then crawled out. The warriors followed him.

Fargo watched them dress and prepare to escort him to the hill on which he would stand. Iron Face bent and beckoned him to come out. As Fargo crawled through the opening, a bearskin fell over his head. From this moment until he again entered the lodge four days hence, he could not look another person in the eyes, nor they into his.

Long Bow served as his guide. He walked in front of Fargo, close enough so Fargo could see his feet at all times. They forded the stream, which felt good, then began ascending. At that point, Fargo knew Iron Face was taking him up Medicine Wheel Mountain. He tried to remember the site where he'd received so much pain, but the details were few and vague at best. He quit thinking about it and watched Long Bow's feet nudge larger pebbles off the narrow footpath, thankful for the warrior's consideration.

The upward climb was brutal, taxing his calf muscles. Not once did Iron Face pause for them to catch their breath or rest. Finally they reached the summit. Fargo listened to Iron Face grunt and bark orders to the two warriors. Long Bow's feet appeared before Fargo's. He said, "Follow me. Watch your footing, my friend. One misstep, and it's instant death."

Long Bow led him slowly, cautiously, as though he

feared as much for his own safety as for Fargo's. Fargo soon saw why. The shielding bearskin forced him to look down. The sheets of dark slate they walked on formed a narrow path of steps protected on the left by a column of jagged layers of slate. They moved around the column so closely that Fargo's shoulders rubbed against it.

Halfway around the pillar Long Bow turned right. They stepped onto a wider, safer walkway. Fargo lifted his forearm to raise the bottom of the bearskin enough to partially view the terrain beside the passageway. It fell away gradually, then plunged straight down. The rocky landscape was barren.

After a few safe paces they came to natural steps that led onto a generally flat surface, wide enough to accommodate the two of them. Long Bow halted and turned to face him. "Fargo, we are now on your *owanka*. I will arrange sage to form the northern limit of your place of confinement. Do not cross over the sage."

A large bundle of sage was placed at his feet. Long Bow removed several strands from it and stepped behind Fargo. "I'm making the boundary," he said.

A few seconds later, he spoke again. "A skirt to protect your lower body from the sun is on the ground behind you. Stand still, Fargo. Do not move your feet until after you take off the bearskin. I will call out after we leave, when we can no longer see you. Remove the bearskin at that time. You will hear me shout when we come back for you. That is the warning to cover your head again.

"One final thing, my friend, before I depart. The spirits will test you at least four times. If your heart and soul are right, they will then honor you with a vision, which Iron Face will interpret for you in the sweat lodge. Be strong, Fargo."

Fargo heard him move away and join the others. Iron Face grunted several times, then there was only the sound of the wind. After what seemed an eternity,

Long Bow shouted, "All right, Fargo, it's safe to uncover."

Fargo raised the bearskin. His heart skipped a beat, then pounded. He stood between two misshapen monoliths of uneven layers of slate, the jagged tops of which were at least a head and a half above his own. Before him was a vast expanse, a majestic panorama of snowcapped mountain peaks in the Big Horn Range. The slate surface on which he stood ended abruptly a pace away. He took a half-step forward and looked down over the edge. The sheer drop-off fell thousands of feet. Fargo sucked in a breath, stepped back, and turned to look behind him.

He stood on a ledge about his length and twice his shoulder width. The sage boundary stretched across the back of the ledge, where the lowering steps began. The steps led down to a walkway at the far end of which rose the slate column. Not too far west of it he saw a funnel-shaped depression in the center of which gaped a small but jagged-edged opening.

Behind the slate pillar was the Medicine Wheel, which no one knew who had constructed or when. He estimated the wheel's diameter at slightly less than fifty feet. The outer, circular rim of stacked pieces of white slate stood no more than a foot and a half high.

The ageless rim was interrupted in five places by mounds of stones arranged about two feet wide and a foot high. Two of the mounds formed a gateway in the north. One each of the other three stood in the other three directions. In the center of the wheel stood a fifth mound of stones. From it emanated twenty-eight equally spaced single layers of stone that connected to the rim. Between each spoke the soil was smooth.

A lone cedar tree flourished in the rocky terrain a short distance southeast of the Medicine Wheel.

Fargo knew the bundle of sage had been left for him to spread on the ledge, to purify it and himself. He arranged it accordingly, then lay the bearskin on it and faced west to offer his first prayer.

"Grandfather, it is I, Skye Fargo, a pitiful human

being, who prays to you. Grandfather, I ask for you to give me the strength and stamina needed while crying for a vision. Help keep my senses open and alert to receive it. And, Grandfather, please protect me from all harm. These few things I pray for, Grandfather."

He turned and pointed the pipe stem north and repeated the prayer. Twice more he prayed to the Grandfathers in the east and south. He pointed the stem straight up, tilted his face skyward, and prayed to the Great Spirit, after which he touched the end of the stem to the ledge and prayed to Mother Earth.

"O Maka Ina, from whom all life springs and is sustained, I beg you to somehow quench my thirst and keep this ledge and mountain steady. Comfort me when I tire. Send cool breezes in the sunrays and warm ones during the cold of night. Show me what you will, Maka Ina, and keep me safe."

Finished with his initial prayers to the six directions, he wrapped and tied the bloodred buckskin skirt around his waist. Then he began the next round of series of prayers that would continue uninterrupted until Long Bow shouted to announce they were returning, or until he collapsed from fatigue. To collapse would be disastrous, for in his delirium, which would surely come, he could easily roll off his sanctuary. He knew Iron Face hoped that would happen.

He was still praying when the sun lowered and cast the ledge in heavy shadows. Before him were the illuminated snowcapped peaks far in the south. As though by magic their brilliance simply vanished, replaced by faint, dark outlines. In that dark instant the spirits tested him.

From behind him came a high-pitched squeaking that slammed against his left shoulder blade, caromed off, and flitted south. He spun and stared into the black void consuming the pillar and Medicine Wheel. A cloud of bats attacked him. He knocked them from his hair and body, snatched up the bearskin, pulled it over him, and sank to his knees. By the hundreds bats hit the protective covering or clung to it. Their incessant squeaking and relentless efforts to work their way inside with him went on until dawn's early light drove them away.

Fargo stood and pulled the bearskin off. He glimpsed the trailing edge of the swarming bats swirling down into the funnel, then he faced west and started another day of prayers. There was no cool breeze in the sun's rays. By noon blisters formed on his shoulders, back, and chest. Neither did any warmth come during the cold of the second night. Something else did.

Thousands of tarantulas and scorpions invaded his *owanka*. They scattered his sage, crawled all over him, up the sides of the monoliths, only to drop onto him. He willed himself to ignore them and kept on praying hard and fast to the Grandfathers.

He received no vision. Neither did the maddening tarantulas and scorpions go away. They stayed with him and on him until well after high noon of the third day, when in the blink of an eye they vanished.

Mother Earth favored him with a gentle breeze, cool and refreshing at first, then it grew cold and intensified. Dark, ugly clouds appeared on the southern horizon. He watched them form into a wall that raced toward him. He braced himself for the onslaught. A freezing wind roared in, blew the sage away, then the bearskin. He struggled to hold on to the pipe, which the furious gusts tried to wrench from his grasp. He went numb from the icy wind.

His teeth chattered while he prayed, "O Grandfathers, Great Spirit, and Maka Ina, I beg you not to hurt me or let me hurt myself. I am not leaving my *owanka*, so test me all you want. I am crying for a vision. Please show it to me, now."

He received no vision. The icy wind blasted his body until sunset. When it died, a warm wind replaced it. Fargo looked down and saw the bed of sage was as before, not one piece missing. The bearskin, too, was as before.

Sometime during the night—he didn't know when; the stars and moon had disappeared—the warm breeze turned warmer and warmer and soon became so hot that he sweated heavily. Finally the air was hotter than an oven. Fargo felt his hair curling; it became hard for him to breathe.

Suddenly, flames burst forth all about the site. Each of the stone mounds at the Medicine Wheel glowed fiery red and started to pulsate. They resembled brains about to burst. Fire consumed the pillar. A geyser of flame shot out of the funnel and stabbed high in the inky void. Flames cavorted in and around the hardy cedar.

A lilting, anguished voice from afar called his name. "Who are you?" he shouted. "What do you want?"

The voice strengthened. "I want you. I need you. Now."

Fargo gasped. Melody Abbott was coming to him. "No, Melody! Stay away from me. We cannot look at each other. I am crying for a vision."

He watched her slink around the fiery pillar and stop midway on the connecting path. Sweat streamed down her naked body. She lay on her back with her feet to him and started squirming toward the steps. At the lower step she raised and parted her legs. Her hot, dripping slot opened wide. She coaxed him to her, moaning, "Take me, Mr. Fargo . . . take me, now. Come and I will make you happy."

"No," he cried. "Go away and leave me alone. Don't tempt me, woman. Can't you see I am crying for a vision to show me where to find your husband? Go away, I say."

But Melody Abbott didn't go away. Neither did the flames. She came and rubbed her nakedness all over him, front and backside.

He forced himself to turn away. She screamed, "Watch me, damn you! I'm getting ready for you. Don't be afraid to take me. Julian is dead."

It went on until dawn of the fourth day. With the first glimmer of light all the flames flickered out. The unbearable hotness went away. He started to shiver. When he forced himself to turn and look behind him, everything was as before the temptation. Melody had vanished. He was gripping the pipe tightly. He pointed it west and started praying.

In late afternoon a raging storm struck. Mighty bolts of multicolored lightning stabbed down out of the roiling black clouds, struck, and exploded all around him. The pillar sizzled, the mountain shook. Thunder boomed and rumbled in from the vast expanse. A deluge fell on the mountaintop. An angry stream of muddy water boiled out of the Medicine Wheel, slammed around the column, sloshed down the walkway and up the steps, then cascaded over the lip of the ledge. Fargo struggled to keep his footing in the torrent of muddy water.

He was exhausted when the furious storm abated and finally disappeared. Panting, he pointed the pipe stem west and prayed, "Grandfather, I am crying for a vision."

That night a blizzard blasted out of the north. The screaming wind drove monstrous snowflakes parallel to the ground. Conestogas, California flatbeds, Owenboros, and many other types of wagons shot over the mountaintop and tumbled into the vast expanse. The vision site quickly filled with driven snow. Fargo stood chest-deep in it. He faced west and prayed.

Just before dawn an eerie silence gripped the mountain. The air became deathly still, as though Mother Earth held her breath. The morning star flared and drew his attention. He watched it move to due south to hover high above the snowcapped peaks.

The bright star pulsated four times, then went out. The lightening sky turned jet-black. He gripped the bowl tighter, aimed the stem south, and said, "Show it to me."

A blue hole appeared in the void. He watched it expand greatly. The blue hole suddenly changed to pure white. Voices wailed. He saw the number seven. Two wolves, one blue with a yellow head, the other off-white with a bloodred head, streaked into the hole from the east, ran across it, and vanished in the west.

Both gripped small pouches in their teeth. When the wolves left, a coiled snake filled the hole. The snake stared at Fargo, flicked its forked tongue, then struck.

As the monstrous mouth opened to devour Fargo, Long Bow shouted, "Cover up, Fargo."

Fargo blinked. Dawn had broken on a gorgeous morning. The soft-blue sky was clear, the distant peaks beautiful. He sighed, faced each direction, saying, "Thank you, Grandfather." Then he draped the bear-skin over his head and waited.

Back in camp, as Fargo crawled through the lodge's door, Long Bow lifted the bearskin from him. Fargo moved to sit in the west. Long Bow and Has No Pony took their positions in the south. Iron Face eased inside and sat by the door. He stared at Fargo, who kept his gaze fixed on the pipe's bowl.

Seven stones came in, then the geode of water. The flap lowered. The Crow started singing. Iron Face dumped all the water onto the arranged stones. Murderously moist heat filled the lodge. Fargo willed himself not to fall over. The last song ended. Iron Face spoke briefly.

Long Bow said, "The spirits are here, Fargo. They will tell the medicine man all that happened and what you saw at the sacred Medicine Wheel. He will tell me, and I will tell you. Relax and listen carefully, for nothing will be repeated."

For the next ten hot minutes Fargo heard Iron Face grunt repeatedly. Finally he spoke to Long Bow and gave him time to repeat what he said before continuing.

Fargo learned he had indeed received a vision, a lengthy one. The bombardment of bats, the fire, storm, legion of tarantulas and scorpions, and the blizzard were imaginary tests. His seductress would succeed. He was destined to see the ghosts of many wagons. The white hole meant much snow. The wolves were two men. The number seven represented as many people, their wailings indicated sadness over a loss. He would not find Julian Abbott. The snake was Shoshoni spirits. The pouches held white men's money. It took Iron Face and Long Bow more than an hour to tell the entire vision.

The flap lifted. Fresh air displaced the steam. A burning twig was handed in. Fargo removed the ball of sage from the pipe's bowl. Long Bow touched the twig's flame to the tobacco. They all smoked the pipe, each in his own turn, till only ashes remained. Fargo took the pipe apart, knocked the ashes onto the stones, and handed the two parts to Iron Face. Iron Face nodded and crawled out.

Outside, Fargo drank water before he dressed. Long Bow handed him a hunk of venison. They waited to talk until after all the others had left. Long Bow asked, "Are you strong enough to fight Has No Pony?"

Around a mouthful of venison, Fargo muttered, "Hope so. Has he said when and where?"

"No. But it will happen within the hour. He's eager to kill you. Iron Face insists. You weren't expected to survive the hill. Iron Face sat in this lodge all the time you were up there. He prayed bad medicine on you."

"It didn't work," Fargo said. "Actually, I feel sorry for the man. Did Has No Pony say what method?"

"No. But he prefers knives."

"Is he any good with one?"

"Very."

"Is Melody behaving?"

"Concerned is more like it. She's been helping the women. And she befriended two of the Shoshoni women we brought back. They seem to like her."

Fargo downed the last of the venison, dragged the back of his hand across his mouth, and said he was ready.

It seemed nearly all of the people, certainly the warriors, had assembled to watch the fight. They pushed through the crowd. Has No Pony stood waiting for them outside his tepee. He'd removed all his clothing and adornments except the buckskin apron. A length of coiled rope lay on the ground at his feet. And he held a bone-handled knife big enough and sharp enough to kill a grizzly.

Fargo stared into Has No Pony's eyes while walking toward him. When he stopped, less than six inches separated their noses. Maintaining his penetrating eye contact, Fargo told Long Bow, "Tell him I'm ready."

Long Bow translated. Has No Pony nodded once, picked up the rope, and strode toward the stream. The gathering chorused a gasp. Chief Fights Plenty took Fargo by the elbow, but spoke to Long Bow. "My father says to tell you it is no dishonor for a man who suffered your ordeal with the spirits to demand time to regain his strength. I think he wants you—"

Fargo's upraised hand stopped him short. He smiled at the chief and said, "Say that while I understand and thank him, I must bring this bad blood to a swift conclusion."

The chief sighed and walked to the stream with them. Halfway there, Melody ran up and grabbed Fargo. "Where are you going?" she demanded. "I want to get out of here."

"Me too," Fargo replied wryly. "Are you coming to watch the big fight?"

"No! I mean, yes. Oh, God, he'll kill you. I just know he will."

"What are you afraid of? That you'll get stuck here?"

"Mr. Fargo, I hate you. I hope he does kill you. Go on. See if I care."

He touched the brim of his hat and continued forward. People were scattered all along both banks. Has No Pony had selected a wide stretch where the water flowed nearly knee-deep. He stood in the middle of the stream. Fargo pulled off his boots and stripped to the waist, then drew his Arkansas toothpick and waded out to his adversary.

Has No Pony tied one end of the rope to his own left wrist and handed the other end to Fargo. Fargo tied it to his left also. Has No Pony motioned for them to step back till the rope was taut. Fargo did, and saw the rope was about six feet long. He jerked on it suddenly. Has No Pony fell facedown in the water and sprang up sputtering and slashing thin air with the knife. Fargo laughed, but gave him time to get set.

The warrior was furious, raging mad. He jerked the rope and slashed. Fargo dodged the gleaming blade and slashed back. For the next ten minutes they fought all through the stretch of water; they tugged on the rope, parried and thrust, danced and dodged away, kicked and slapped water at each other. Finally Fargo saw the way to overcome his opponent: Has No Pony favored a backhand slash.

Fargo maneuvered him into position where the man could have a clear backhanded shot at him. The long blade sliced through the air. Fargo's left hand shot out, grabbed the knife hand, and twisted. Has No Pony's hand opened and the knife dropped into the water. Fargo jerked on the rope. Caught off-balance, the warrior went down. Fargo was on him in an instant. They came up with the tip of Fargo's knife on Has No Pony's throat and Fargo gripping the warrior's left wrist. Their eyes met and locked. Fargo saw resignation, but no sign of defeat in Has No Pony's.

He moved the cutting edge of the knife to the man's left palm and sliced just deep enough to draw blood. Then he sliced his own left palm and gripped it to Has No Pony's, signifying they were now blood brothers and there could be no more fighting between them. Has No Pony stood and embraced him. Iron Face was heard to groan.

That night, while eating more of the delicious venison in their tepee, Melody asked when they would leave. "I would like to take those two Shoshoni maidens with us," she added. "This is no place for any of them, although the other four seem not to mind being in captivity."

"Don't be a rescuer," Fargo muttered. "They would only slow us down."

"No, they wouldn't," she pressed.

"Oh? Riding two on a horse would."

"They could ride their own horses. Chief What's-his-name would give them to you if you asked. Even I can see he likes you."

"No, he wouldn't. Indians will give up their women before they would a pony. Get some sleep. We leave at the crack of dawn."

Resigned that he wouldn't help the maidens, she asked, "Did you get a vision?"

"Yes, and you wouldn't like to hear about it. It's bedtime." He started undressing.

He was loosening his shirt buttons when a female's piercing scream penetrated the entire encampment. Both he and Melody shot to their feet and sprang for the door. They looked out, saw mounted riders pounding into the camp from all directions.

"Indians," Fargo said. "They're after Crow women and ponies."

As he spoke a warrior slid from his pony and ran inside a tepee. Within seconds several tepees burst into flames. Crow women ran screaming for safety, their warrior men into the fray on foot. The campsite soon boiled with dirt and dust, and other tepees were put to the torch.

Fargo told her, "Follow me. I'll get us to safety on the stream." He yanked her outside.

She wrenched free of his grasp and yelled, "No, I have to help those poor Shoshoni girls!" She started running toward a tepee.

"Dammit, this isn't our fight," he shouted. When she didn't stop or look back, he mumbled, "Well, shit," and hurried to catch her.

Melody led the two slim maidens out of the tepee just as Fargo arrived. He took one look at the women's terrified faces and said, "Come on."

They wove through mounted riders fending off Crow warriors to get to their tepee. After gathering up their gear, he chased the women to the corral and made their horses ready to ride. He was amazed the Crow had left their ponies unguarded until he saw two dead warriors sprawled on the ground. The attackers apparently intended to massacre the Crow and take the ponies at their leisure. He didn't have to tell the young women to take ponies; they were already on them and ready to head out.

As they were leaving the corral, a warrior gripping a hatchet staggered toward them and collapsed. Fargo wheeled the Ovaro and went back to fetch a pony. "Hurry, Mr. Fargo," Melody shouted. "They're coming this way."

He scooped the downed man from the ground and draped him over the pony's back, then headed for the stream, where he turned and rode west.

Melody said, "Thank you, Mr. Fargo. I might end up liking you yet."

He vaguely heard her, for he wondered if they had escaped their stalkers. He doubted it. After all, greed was a powerful motivating force, especially to westerners, who saw no fault in it.

Fargo rode on into the night.

10

Shortly before sunup Fargo reined the Ovaro to a halt and told the others they were stopping to sleep. He lifted the unconscious warrior from the pony and stretched him out on the ground to find his wound. He felt a lump the size of a bantam hen's egg on the back of the young man's head. Several bruises showed on his back and left thigh. Fargo signed for the girls to look after the man, whom he reckoned was Shoshoni.

While Melody made a fire, he unsaddled the horses and spread their bedrolls. Then he made a lean-to for the Indians. The young women picked prairie grass and arranged it beneath the lean-to for them to lie on.

The warrior regained consciousness, fighting for his life. Both shrieking Shoshoni women fell back to escape his flailing fists. They quickly collected their wits and started shouting at him. It was obvious to Fargo they were censuring him severely. He signed to the confused warrior, "We come in peace. You are among friends."

The man's nod triggered a painful grimace. He felt over his head and found the knot on it. After inspecting the rest of his body, he engaged the two young females in conversation. Fargo let it go on for a while before signing to him, "What is your name? What are theirs?"

"Fast Elk," the warrior signed back. He touched one of the maidens. "Blue Sage." The other was Laughing Bear. Both were from Chief Washakie's winter camp on the Wind River far to the south.

Fargo brewed coffee, which the Shoshoni refused to

drink, but did partake of Melody's trail meal. After eating, Fargo reclined on his bedroll for much-needed sleep.

Melody, however, wanted to talk. "Mr. Fargo, where are we? How much farther is it to a town where I can purchase a few things and sleep at least one night on a real bed?"

"Well, ma'am," he sighed, "it's a hell of a long way to a real bed. We're on the western slope of the Big Horn Mountain Range." He listened to her clean their plates.

As he shut his eyes again, she asked, "Where are we going?"

"Seattle."

"I know that, Mr. Fargo. I meant before we get there."

He sat up. "Look around you. You'll see more of the same between here and Seattle. If you wanted the comforts of home, you should have joined a wagon train of settlers going west. Now, don't talk to me anymore. I'm dog-tired from standing in one place for four days, fighting with Has No Pony, then getting you all out of a bad scrape. Don't say another word until I wake up. If you do, so help me, I'll scalp you and leave your carcass for buzzards to fight over." He rolled onto his stomach.

He awakened to see a setting sun. Melody sat on her bedroll, staring at him through the fire. "I hate you, Mr. Fargo. You're a big bully."

He yawned and smacked his lips. "Well, honey, you're no prize, either," he said sleepily. He stood and began to saddle the pinto.

"Are we leaving?" she asked. "It's nearly dark."

"Day or night, ma'am, makes no difference to me." He gestured for the Shoshoni to mount up. By the time he secured his bedroll and saddlebags to the pinto, Melody had her stallion ready to ride. He shot her a wink. Through an easy grin he said, "You did well. I'm impressed by your remarkable speed." He pulled on the fleece-lined coat Charley had given him, and suggested she get into hers.

"Why?" she asked, looking around. "There's not a cloud in the sky."

"Do what you want, ma'am."

Two hours later a raw north wind hit them. Fargo halted and dismounted. So did Melody to get her coat out of the bedroll. Fargo removed his shirt and gave it to Fast Elk. He told Melody to give him hers also.

"I'll freeze," she complained.

"No, you won't, but he might. Take it off and give it to him."

"What about those poor little girls?"

"They get our bedrolls." He handed his to Blue Sage.

The cold wind strengthened during the night. At dawn he halted beside dense ground cover. After unsaddling the Ovaro, he started digging in the loose soil with his knife. The Shoshoni realized what he was doing. They dropped onto their knees and dug with their hands. Melody asked, "Mr. Fargo, what are you doing?"

"We're preparing a warm bed. It's time you got your hands dirty. Start breaking dry limbs from that thicket."

In short order they had carved out a long, wide shallow pit. Fast Elk scooped out the remaining loose soil and rocked back on his haunches. Fargo nodded to them. They stacked the firewood in it. Fargo set it to blaze.

While it burned, they collected more wood and added it to the fire, then sat around the pit and watched the wood reduce to coals.

Fargo signed instructions to the Shoshoni. They started gathering anything small and green while Melody watched Fargo erect a lean-to over the pit. The greenery was spread and packed over the bed of embers.

Fargo opened the bedrolls and laid them over the green mat. "Today we bundle," he told Melody.

"I'm sleeping with the girls," she hissed.

"Wouldn't have it any other way, honey." He took off his coat and reclined on one end of the makeshift but warm bed, then gestured for Fast Elk to lay beside him. When the warrior was in place, Fargo spread half the open coat over him.

Melody got between Blue Sage and Laughing Bear and shared hers with them. As Fargo's eyes closed, she said, "You're pretty smart, Mr. Fargo."

"Uh, huh," he muttered. Drifting into sleep, he wondered if their trackers were out there and had seen the fire. He hadn't seen any of them since leaving Fights Plenty's camp.

Fargo had everybody up and riding single-file at midafternoon. The leading edge of dull-gray clouds loomed in the north. The ominous arc stretched from the eastern to western horizons. They watched it move toward them and finally blot out the sun. Fargo told them to continue riding in a straight line, that he would search for natural shelter in the rolling terrain on their left.

After searching for nearly an hour, he spotted the entrance to a cave low on the north side of a rocky hillock. He dismounted and checked it out. The tight opening led into a space he doubted would hold the five of them. The ceiling was extremely low, the back wall no more than six feet from the ragged entrance. He threw out the rocks and larger pebbles, then smoothed the bumpy floor with his hands. He decided they might wedge in if they laid close together on their sides.

As he mounted to go get them, the blizzard struck with an intensity he'd never known. Before he could ride out of the depression he could not see his hand in front of his face.

Consumed completely in the mass of white, he could not discern his way back to the others. He moved on gut instinct, hoping to cross or see their path. After an hour of trying, he decided it was hopeless. It would be up to Fast Elk to cope with their situation. He turned back to retrace his movements and try to find the cave again.

An hour passed, then another before the pinto knickered and started down a slope. The Ovaro's knicker was answered by another. Fargo gave the stallion free rein. It went straight to an Appaloosa standing in front of the opening with its rump to the wind. Fargo dismounted, removed his saddle and saddlebags, grabbed his bedroll, poked it all inside, then crawled in.

Victoria Ellison purred, "Cold as all Billy hell out there, isn't it, big man? Come on in. We'll snuggle up to generate some heat, else we'll freeze to death."

He didn't argue with the willowy ash blonde. He crammed his stuff next to hers and started to spread his bedroll, but she stopped him. "Wait a minute, big man. I'll get out of mine so you can lay yours on it. We can't make any heat tucked in alone." She crawled out.

When he had his in place and open, she squirmed inside. He undressed, then got in with her. "I want you to know I'm damn glad you saw me find this hole."

"Yes, now you find mine." She put his cold hands between her thighs. "Big man, I don't have the widow's breasts, but you're welcome to nurse on mine."

Without removing a hand from her warm spot, he bent and searched for a nipple with his lips. They found champagne-glass-sized mounds, both firm, with nipples round as a half-penny. He rolled first one then the other between his teeth. She moaned, "Jesus, am I ever lucky. Way the hell out in nowhere, in a hole in the ground, with a big man's teeth nibbling me into ecstasy. Don't quit. Bite so I'll know this is really happening."

He bit gently, she gasped delightedly, then he sucked in most of the breast and circled it with his tongue. Her thighs clamped harder on his hands and she squealed, "Get its twin too. Jesus, you're driving me crazy."

When he moved onto the other one, he felt her fingers twist his hair. She helped him roll his head to work more of the breast inside his mouth. "I'm hot," she cried. "Oh, Jesus, am I ever. Take it anytime you're ready. God knows it's as ready as it will ever get."

She squirmed under him and parted her legs. When he felt up her hot swollen lips with his middle finger, she dug her fingernails into his rump, raised her hips, and gasped, "That's so good . . . so beautiful." He parted the lips and probed. Squirming her ass, she shrieked, "Deeper! Go all the way. Oh, Jesus, Jesus, Jesus, I see shooting stars."

He favored her a minute longer before replacing the finger with his throbbing staff. With the penetration, she sucked in a breath through clenched teeth. He felt her long legs wrap over his and cling tightly to gain leverage to meet his initial deep plunge. She wiggled to increase her thrill and force the pleasure-giving organ to find new depths.

In all the way, he gyrated his hips. She murmured, "Oh, Jesus, big man . . . where have you been all my life? You've ruined me for any other man, but I don't care. Go faster . . . please go faster. That's it, that's it. Aaaayeeeiii!"

She bit him on both shoulders. She bit his neck and she wet-massaged his left ear with her swirling hot tongue. He thrust faster and deeper. She raked his back and screamed, "More! Give me more! Don't stop . . . please don't ever stop!"

He took her by the rump and pulled up and pounded into her deepest recess. She started gasping, "Oh, oh, oh . . . you're on the bottom . . . and it's wonderful. My brain is swirling . . . I'm in heaven . . . Jesus, don't stop."

He felt his gusher rising to surface. She sensed it coming and begged, "Not yet! Wait for me. Wait for me." He felt her spasm, pulled her crotch tighter to him, and let it come. She whimpered, "Oh, Jesus, that's good. So damn wonderful. I needed this. Oh,

God, how I needed you, big man. I know it's over, but don't take it out. Jesus, but you're powerful."

But he did withdraw. They lay panting, bathed in each other's sweat for a long time before she unlocked her legs from around his. Her long fingers framed his head and she kissed him passionately, openmouthed. Finally she broke the kiss and cuddled next to him. She was silent for a while, then whispered, "I love you. You made me feel like a woman for the first time in a long, long time. Melody Abbott doesn't deserve a handsome man like you. Am I not better at making you happy than she?"

"I wouldn't know," he answered. "She hates me, or claims she does."

She responded by hugging him tightly. After a long moment she said, "We don't need her, you and I. We can find it without any help from her."

"Find what?" He knew the answer, but wanted her to say it.

Feeling over his biceps, she whispered, "You know, the payroll."

"Oh, I see. That's what everybody's out here for? Money?"

"Certainly. She hasn't mentioned it? Damn, I bet she hasn't. It would be like that cunning bitch not to tell you that's why she hired you. Seattle, my ass. She's as greedy as the rest of us."

"She hopes to find her husband or learn what happened to him."

"Ha! That's what she says, huh? She knows he's dead. That payroll is up for grabs, big man. It's out here somewhere. I know it is. Hell, I can smell green money from a mile away. We're close to it. I know we are. What's west of here, anyhow?"

"More of what we've been through. More gorgeous to my way of thinking. The Rockies are in front of us."

"I knew it," she cried. "Selman mentioned the Rockies to me once. 'Darling,' he said, 'we could get lost from civilization in that Rocky Mountain high country in Wyoming Territory and make out forever.' That's where he took it. The lying bastard's hiding out in high country, waiting for the army to forget all about losing their payroll."

"Maybe so," Fargo replied, "but right now all I want is some sleep. Thanks for the unexpected warm-up, Victoria. I'll see you in the morning."

"I adore making morning love."

"Is that a promise?"

"Wait and see."

He drifted to sleep wondering where Fast Elk and the others were and if they were alive.

11

In midmorning the early-winter storm abated. Fargo crawled out of the haven and trudged through shin-deep snow to see about their horses. Both stood among sheltering rocks. The Ovaro knickered. Fargo brushed the snow from both animal's backs and faces, then returned to the cave. "Wake up, Victoria. It's time to saddle up."

Victoria twisted inside the warm bedroll and muttered sleepily, "So soon? Can't we stay here until spring? What about our making love?"

He got his saddle and tack. "Honey, when the hard part of winter sets in, you'll think this was spring. Get dressed and bring your stuff to the rocks." He headed for the horses.

Fifteen minutes later they rode out of the rocky shelter. He reined the Ovaro west. He had Victoria ride in a straight line while he rode lengthy switchbacks to find Melody and the Indians' tracks. Progress through the white mantle was slow and often dangerous. After two hours of searching for them, he decided they were either dead or had moved so far away he'd never find them. He abandoned his search and caught up with Victoria.

At noon the trailing edge of the dull-gray storm clouds passed overhead. A warm sun beamed down from an azure sky, but its rays had little effect on the freezing temperature that clung to the ground and filled the air.

At sunset he found shelter for them and their mounts in rocks on the east side of a mountain. While Victoria made a fire, he erected a lean-to. They ate a trail meal, added wood to the fire, then retired for the night. Again they slept naked together. She laid on him and under him half the night. Neither got much sleep.

A sudden change in temperature snapped Fargo's eyes open. He poked the rest of his head out of the bedroll and glanced at the starry night. Warm wind smacked his face; a Chinook had blasted in over the Rockies. He knew the hot wind would transform the all-white scenery into a muddy quagmire within hours. He drew back inside, snuggled against Victoria's backside, and went back to sleep.

The Chinook lingered two days. During that time, Fargo tried repeatedly to find the others, but saw no sign of them. He and Victoria made good progress, and Fargo had no problem providing venison for their meals. On the third day, they were well into the Rocky Mountain high country when the Chinook gave way to a cold front.

Fargo detected a trace of smoke in the cold wind. "Keep your eyes open," he told her. "Be alert. We are near a Shoshoni camp site."

He angled the pinto into the wind. As they rode farther into it, the smell of smoke became more pronounced. Soon it became visible, wafting through the forest of towering Douglas firs. Soft laughter of children at play signaled the camp would come into view any moment.

Fargo reined to a halt and instructed her. "We're too far north for Chief Washakie to be present this time of year. He's supposed to be camped on the Wind River. If we're fortunate, this chief will treat us same as Washakie and let us pass without harm. But, the truth is, I don't know what we will find here. I'll do the talking. Remember to show respect by keeping your eyes lowered." When she nodded, he nudged the Ovaro forward at a walk.

They broke out of the tree line into a small clearing. Fargo counted fifteen tepees, six in the open space, the others among the firs. A sheet of canvas lay draped over what looked like a small-bore carriage-mounted army cannon. He didn't see the wagon.

There were other things that didn't belong among tepees, all totally incongruous to this setting, the Indian way of life. Iron stoves, some with flues sticking straight up, stood out in the open, as did several cast iron kettles used for boiling dirty clothes. A washboard leaned against a tree trunk. Coils of baling wire, too many to count, lay rusting on the ground. Kegs and barrels were strewn about.

The children spotted them first and fled to women tending fires outside the tepees. The women were quick to shout the alarm, then hurried their youngsters to safety, away from Fargo and Victoria. Fargo halted and waited with his hands on his saddle horn.

Within seconds armed warriors surrounded them. Fargo took his hands away from the saddle horn to show they were empty. He told Victoria to do the same. A warrior motioned for them to dismount.

The gathering parted to clear a path for two men who emerged from the largest tepee in the clearing. The shorter, older man wore all the trappings of the medicine man.

The man striding a half-pace in front of him had to be the chief. He wore buckskin pants and moccasins. A magnificent bone choker adorned his strong neck, and silver bracelets encircled his arms above the elbows. On his head was an army officer's hat with two eagle feathers, one on either side of the crown.

Fargo raised his right hand in peace. Both men stopped two paces away and studied him and Victoria from head to foot for a long moment.

In broken English the chief asked, "You are Trailsman?"

Relieved, Fargo nodded.

The chief continued. "Why were you with the Crow?"

More relieved Fargo answered, "We come in peace. I look for two white men, both bad. It is said they came this way during the summer season. Did you see them?"

The chief didn't answer his question, but the medicine man did obliquely. Fargo saw his eyes flare. It also told him the man understood English well enough to follow the drift of conversation.

The chief said, "I am Chief Red Horn. Come, Trailsman." He grunted to the warriors, turned, and strode toward a tepee slightly smaller and left of the one he had come from. The warriors relaxed their vigilance. The medicine man, Lame Hawk, stepped aside for Fargo and Victoria to pass, then fell in behind them.

Fast Elk and Melody sat behind the fire inside the tepee. She glanced up at Fargo, then down just as quickly when he and Victoria stepped inside and paused for Red Horn to tell them where to sit.

Red Horn sat cross-legged on buffalo robes at the east side of the fire. He gestured for them to sit on those spread on the west so they faced him.

As he found his place, Fargo glanced about the interior. Unlike the Sioux, Red Horn clearly practiced materialism. Items collected from settlers on the Bozeman Trail hung from the tepee poles or lay on the ground. Among them he saw mirrors, a tin washbasin, two muskets, a washboard, and a pair of women's high-top shoes. Behind Melody stood Red Horn's staff. Among the black-haired scalps tied to it, two were different; one was red, the other blond. Fargo wondered if Red Horn's army hat once covered Lieutenant Julian Abbott's head, but knew his curiosity would have to wait.

Red Horn said, "Fast Elk told how you saved him and two of the women from Washakie's camp. That is good, Trailsman. You are our friend. Two of my warriors were killed by the Crow. The warriors' uncles took their women as relatives. Their tepees are empty. You and the white women can live in one while you are with us. Fast Elk will take you to it."

Fargo said, "Thank you, my friend, but I prefer to

rest alone. Perhaps they can share the other empty tepee."

Red Horn looked at him for a few seconds as though amazed by the request, then grunted and nodded. He reclined, indicating this meeting was over. Fast Elk stood and motioned for the others to do likewise, then preceded them through the tepee door.

Outside, Melody snapped, "Where did you get her? Why did you leave me? What took you so long to get here?" She shot a hard stare at Victoria.

Victoria's swift answer implied more than it said, much more. "I took him for a stroll in my yellow rose garden. Have you learned where the cash is?"

Melody didn't answer.

Fargo asked them, "What color hair do your men have?"

Melody glanced up at him sharply. "Dark blond. Why?"

"Just wondering. How about yours, Victoria?" He was sure of her answer, but wanted it verified.

"Selman was redheaded, rusty-colored."

He noticed she used the past tense, which probably meant she had seen Selman's scalp hanging on the staff. His demise apparently didn't upset her. She made the verification as though totally unconcerned.

Fast Elk led the women to their tepees first. Walking to the other tepee, he pointed to the sky and used sign language to say a storm was imminent. Fargo followed his point and agreed, adding it would be a monster.

His was a sixteen-pole tepee, average for a couple without children. With the exception of several robes for bedding and a hanging bag of drinking water, everything else had been removed. He went outside and collected an armload of firewood. After making a small fire, he undressed and lay down to nap.

Snowflakes hitting on his eyelids awakened him. He looked up at the top spiral of poles. The vent flaps were facing into the wind. The heat rising from his fire was not sufficient to keep the windblown snow out.

He added a few small sticks to the fire, dressed, and went outside to move the flap poles.

The late-afternoon sky was dark gray, and the wind was strengthening. He worked in finger-deep snow repositioning the two long lodgepole pines connected to the vent flaps. He adjusted them to face away from the wind, then closed them somewhat. He gathered another armload of firewood. Back inside, he checked for draft, found it satisfactory, put a piece of slow-burning oak on the fire, undressed again, and went back to sleep.

Wind howling through the treetops roused him two hours later. This time when he looked skyward, it was pitch-black. He lay listening to the wind for a while, then got up and looked out the tepee entrance. Snow at least a foot deep covered the ground, and more was driving in. Visibility was so limited that he couldn't see any of the other tepees. He closed the lower flap and withdrew to the warmth of the robes.

As the night lengthened, the blizzard intensified. Dawn brought precious little relief. By noon the worst blasts had passed overhead and roared south. The fierce wind slackened. Fargo ventured out into the knee-deep snow to relieve himself and see about the Ovaro. Like all the Indian ponies the pinto stood with his rump against the wind. Fargo brushed the snow off the pinto's face and stroked his powerful neck. Melody's black stallion stood next to a gray dappled mare. The gray had not been there when he unsaddled the Ovaro.

He went to Fast Elk's tepee, slapped the door flap twice, and shouted above the wind, "Trailsman!"

Fast Elk pushed the flap back. After peering out at the snow-covered ground, he waved Fargo inside. Two women poked their heads out from buffalo robes to see what was up. They watched Fargo sit and warm his hands over the fire.

Fast Elk broke two dry tree limbs into small sections and put them on the fire. In sign language, he asked,

"Is there a problem? Do you need a woman to keep you warm? Will the white women not warm you?"

Fargo signed, "There is a new horse in the corral. A gray mare. Is it a Shoshoni horse?"

Fast Elk shook his head, then spoke to the women. Fargo watched him rise and get dressed. Fast Elk signed, "Come. We go see the chief."

One of Red Horn's three women pushed the flap back. After Fast Elk spoke to her, Red Horn said, "Come inside and sit." The woman pushed the flap full open and stepped aside.

Red Horn lay propped on one elbow. A woman lay under the robe next to him. The one who let them in hurried to join the other snuggled under more robes at the back of the tepee. Fargo and Fast Elk sat and warmed their hands. After Fast Elk spoke, Red Horn looked at Fargo and said, "A white woman rode in after dawn. The horse is hers, Trailsman. She is with the other white women."

Fargo suspected the woman was Judith. "How tall is she?" he asked. "And what color hair?"

Red Horn shook his head, then spoke to Fast Elk, who rose and left the tepee.

Red Horn asked, "Why are these white women here, Trailsman? They are not your women?"

"That's correct." Fargo explained how and where he first met them and why he was taking Melody west. He told of finding Victoria after being separated from the others. He decided to mention the others tracking him. "Chief, there are five white men out there. They are armed and dangerous. They have followed us all the way from Fort Hope."

Red Horn grunted and nodded. "Then they will not follow anymore, Trailsman. They are now ice."

Fast Elk slapped the door flap and gave his name. Red Horn told him to enter. Fast Elk sat and spoke to his chief. Red Horn grunted, "He looked at the woman. She stands to his shoulders. Brown hair. Do you know her?"

Fargo nodded.

Red Horn conversed at length with Fast Elk. At the conclusion, the warrior left. Red Horn explained, "I told him to take nine warriors and search for the white men. If they find any, you will be told."

Fargo thanked him and left. He went to the women's tepee and entered unannounced. All three were buried from sight between robes. "All right, ladies, it's time we had a little talk." He squatted and added sticks to their fire.

"Go away, Mr. Fargo," Melody said. "I don't want to talk to you, or anybody else, especially these two."

"No, I want to know what's going on. The chief's sent warriors to bring in those five men, if they aren't frozen. One way or another I intend to get to the bottom of this. What about it, Judith? Victoria?"

Judith squirmed out far enough to look at him. She said, "What's the hurry, big man? Can't this wait till tomorrow or the next day?"

Victoria's voice added, "Besides, you know perfectly well why we're here, doesn't he, Melody?"

Melody sat and looked her way. "I don't care what you say. My husband is out there somewhere. He's hurt."

"Honey," Judith said, chuckling, "your husband is in a cozy saloon with a shapely female on his lap."

Fargo had to restrain Melody from tearing into Judith. "Let go of me, Mr. Fargo," she screeched. "I'll teach her to keep her filthy mouth shut."

"Sit down, Melody," he said. "You're both wrong. The man's dead."

"No," Melody screamed. "Julian is not dead!" She buried herself under robes and started sobbing.

Victoria propped on an elbow and said, "Jesus Christ, Fargo, do something with her, will you? If there's anything I can't stand it's a bawling female." She looked at Melody, but commented to Fargo. "Was that her husband's scalp on the staff?"

Fargo nodded.

Melody screamed, "Julian is not dead!"

Judith said, "Take me to your tepee, Fargo. I'll explain everything to you."

"Tell you what," Fargo began, "I see talking to you three is impossible right now. So I'm going to leave and let you argue or fight, or whatever it is women do to come to a meeting of the minds. When you're ready to sit and calmly discuss things with me, I'll come back. Then I might figure a way out of this for all of us. Seattle is still a hell of a long way off. You better get on a friendly basis or you'll never make it there." He stood, shook his head, and left.

Judith followed as far as her tepee door. She shouted, "I need you, Fargo."

"No," he answered over his shoulder, "you just think you do." He kept walking.

12

Fargo had been sipping coffee off and on for an hour when he heard the warriors return. Within minutes somebody slapped on his door. He opened the flap and looked out. Fast Elk grinned at him. He beckoned the warrior inside and signed, "You found them?"

Fast Elk squatted by the fire. Before warming his hands, he held up two fingers, then signed, "In medicine man's spirit tepee. We go. Chief, come. Much talk."

Fargo poured him a cup of coffee, never expecting the warrior to take it, much less drink the steaming brew. It was rare to find an Indian who had acquired a taste for coffee. To his surprise, Fast Elk guzzled it. He made a terrible face, handed the empty cup back, and indicated that while it tasted horrible, the coffee did warm his insides. Fargo pulled on his heavy coat and headed for the door.

Lame Hawk's spirit tepee was quite large, held up by twenty-five tall lodgepole pine. The twin upper flaps and two feet of the hide covering below them were painted flat black, as was a similar band around the bottom of the tepee. Between the two black bands were multicolored designs and symbols. While Fargo did not know their meanings, he did know they concerned Lame Hawk's medicine. They entered without asking for permission.

A blue-white haze of thick smoke filled the interior. Fargo instantly recognized the aroma carried in the smoke as a combination of sage, flat cedar, and sweetgrass, sacred to most Indians on the Great Plains.

The purifying smoke billowed from half a large sea-shell, an item treasured by medicine men. Lame Hawk was making sure his medicine and many spiritual objects were protected from being fouled by the white men. Fargo knew that throughout this council, Lame Hawk would keep adding more of the mixture to that smoldering.

Lame Hawk sat west of the fire. A vacant position on his left separated him from two elders who sat staring without expression into the flickering flames. Fargo recognized the two white men, Sid and Everett, seated east and slightly south of the fire. Twelve warriors ringed the eastern half of the tepee.

Lame Hawk motioned for Fast Elk to approach and sit on his right. They spoke in low tones and grunts before East Elk signed for Fargo to sit next to Sid.

Ten minutes passed before Chief Red Horn made his entrance. He moved sunwise going to the vacant position. He sat, studied Sid and Everett briefly, then spoke to the warriors nearest the door. Four hurried outside. Red Horn explained, "They go for the white women."

For the next five minutes Red Horn and Lame Hawk conversed in Shoshoni. Occasionally, the medicine man waved his eagle-wing fan over the smoldering mixture in the seashell to excite the smoke and spread it. They fell mute as the warriors returned.

The flap opened. The women entered first. Red Horn had them stand and wait a long moment before saying, "Sit next to that white man." He puckered his lips at Everett.

Red Horn watched their faces while they moved to obey. After puckering toward Melody, he cited an observation. "Why do all of you watch this woman?" When nobody answered, he looked at Sid and said, "Speak."

Sid shrugged, made no comment.

Red Horn shifted his gaze and pucker to Everett. "Speak, white man."

Everett neither shrugged nor replied.

In turn, Red Horn demanded that Victoria and Judith speak up. Neither uttered a word. Both sat still as statues with their chins down and their eyes lowered.

Red Horn told them, "Look at me, foolish white women." When neither did, he said, "I told you to look at me."

Fargo cleared his throat and glanced at the chief. Red Horn nodded permission for him to speak. Fargo turned to the women and said, "Look at him. He's given approval. So do it."

All three tilted their heads up and met Red Horn's gaze. He muttered, "Good. Now speak and answer me."

None did.

Red Horn focused on Melody. "Why do they watch you?"

"I don't know," she answered.

The chief's patience had ended. He stood, drew his knife, and grunted a command to the warriors. As a unit, they stepped forward and grabbed all but Fargo by the hair and jerked their heads back. Victoria and Judith gulped their fear. Melody screamed.

Red Horn moved to stand between them and the fire. As he stared at each of the five upturned faces, he pointed the knife at them menacingly. Finally he said, "No, I will not cut your throats. I will give you to my warriors as slaves. But first, to make sure you cannot speak, I will cut off your tongues." He stepped forward and touched the tip of the knife to Sid's lips.

Sid croaked, "Wait, I'll talk."

Red Horn went down the line, touching each pair of lips with the knife's tip. All swallowed hard and agreed to talk. Red Horn grunted for the warriors to release them, then returned to his place. He started with Sid. "Who are you, white man? Why are you here?"

Sid told his name and explained, "I drove the wagon you attacked last summer. I know it was you because I saw the cannon outside."

"You want the cannon back? You can have it." Red Horn looked at Everett.

Everett said, "I, too, was one of the troopers you ambushed."

Red Horn puckered at Victoria. She said, "I'm here for the money, nothing else."

"What money?" Red Horn asked, and moved his stare to Judith.

She explained quickly, "The army payroll that was in the wagon? You have no use for money, so why not give it to me, and I'll be on my way?"

Red Horn didn't comment. He shifted his gaze to Melody. She said, "Mr. Fargo is taking me to Seattle. I know nothing about money."

"You lie," Everett retorted. He looked at Red Horn and explained, "Her husband was the officer in charge of the payroll detachment."

Red Horn muttered, "All of you lie except this woman." He puckered at Judith. Scanning their faces, he warned, "Say the truth, all of it, or I will strip you naked and stake you to the ground outside, where the spirits will judge if you are to live or die."

Fargo wondered who would break first. Judith did. "I don't want to freeze to death. Tell him, Melody. Tell him the whole sordid truth about why you hired Fargo."

Red Horn stared at Melody and waited. She hesitated momentarily, then apparently decided Red Horn meant what he threatened. "It is true my husband was in charge. His body was not found among the dead. I have reason to believe he is hurt but still alive. I am here to find him. These vultures are welcome to the money. Give it to them and send them away."

Victoria volunteered, "My, er, companion, Selman Davies, was with you during the attack. His body was never found, either. However, I know he is dead. His scalp hangs with her husband's on your staff. I don't know or care why you took it. I'm here to claim Selman's part of the money."

Fargo indicated he wanted to speak. Red Horn nodded his approval. Fargo asked the two men, "What happened? What leads you to believe Mrs. Abbott knows the whereabouts of the payroll? Don't give me any bullshit when you answer. Everett, you go first."

Everett didn't hesitate to reply, "The Shoshoni, this woman's consort, and Lieutenant Abbott made off with everything. The lieutenant faked being wounded. Sid will back me up on that. And the army knows it's true. I was told—ordered is more like it—to say Abbott was wounded and went after the attackers. It was a condition for receiving a so-called medical discharge. I bet Sid was forced to say the same.

"As for why I'm here . . . I got shot up watching after that payroll. So did Sid. Nobody else sitting here shed one drop of their blood for it. Sid and me have every right to that money."

Everett paused and glanced at the women. "I don't know about those other two, but Mrs. Abbott's not telling all she knows."

Fargo questioned her, "What about it, ma'am?"

Everett had more to say. "Mrs. Abbott arranged everything."

Melody blurted, "How dare you accuse me of such a thing! How could I?" She looked to Fargo for support.

Fargo asked Sid, "What's your story?"

Sid nodded slowly. "Only what I saw and the rumors I heard in the hospital. Ev and me, we weren't in the same hospital, but it sounds like he heard much the same as me. What Ev said about the lieutenant acting hurt is true. Don't know about Ev, but I told the major who questioned me exactly what I saw. He told me I was mistaken, that I was too hurt and confused to see things clearly.

"Anyhow, if the lieutenant was in on it—and I'm convinced he was—then his wife knew. When I got out of the hospital, I went to Cincinnati and kept an eye on her."

Fargo pressed him. "You and Everett teamed up?"

Everett answered, "No. I went to Cincinnati too. Sid was already there. He had a room across the street from Mrs. Abbott. I took one in the house next door to her. But Sid and me, we weren't partners. Hell, I thought Sid and Mrs. Abbott were partners." He glanced at Melody and added, "For all I know they are."

Fargo stood and approached Judith. "Okay, honey, let's hear how you got in on this. Start at the beginning."

Judith replied, "I read about it in the newspaper same as everybody else. I was in Kearny, working in Gandy's Saloon. Troopers told me barrack gossip had it those articles weren't altogether true. More than one trooper claimed sweet Melody here dominated her husband, that she knew about the ambush in advance. I believed their tales. So, when Melody showed up at Fort Kearny, I figured it meant she was heading west to meet up with her thieving husband."

Judith glanced at Everett, smiled, and went on. "As luck would have it, the night before the stage left for Fort Hope Everett visited my room. He was drunk. I listened to him blubber about the lieutenant's wife going to the payroll money. Took a while for me to drag it out of him, but he told me all about what he saw during the attack. He even said he'd followed her from Ohio.

"I know enough about holding up stages and . . ." Judith paused to look at Melody. "And conniving women to recognize a setup. I made it a point to catch that stage."

When she fell silent, Victoria said, "Selman wrote and told me everything was going as planned, that he'd see me in St. Joe within two weeks after I read about it in the paper. When I didn't see or hear from him, I knew the bastard had double-crossed me. I didn't know if Melody knew about the theft. On the outside chance that she did, I went to Cincinnati to watch her. My long vigilance from an upstairs room in the boardinghouse on the corner from where she lived finally paid off. You know the rest."

Red Horn grunted for Fargo to sit and listen carefully. His penetrating eyes moved from one to the other as he said, "The white men, Davies and the officer, lied to me. I took their scalps. The money is in the wagon." He puckered toward Judith and continued. "This woman speaks the truth. We have no use for white man's money. All of you can have it."

The five visibly relaxed and exchanged glances.

Judith smiled and said, "Thank you, Chief."

Red Horn chuckled. "No, not me, white woman. Thank Trailsman." He paused and swept his gaze across their faces again, saying, "Shoshoni spirits guard the money you seek. If the spirits want you to have it, they will give it to you, not me."

Everett muttered, "Uh, is it all right for me to ask where your spirits guard it?"

Red Horn's eyes cut to him. "The army wagon is at the far end of the canyon you crossed to come here. Tomorrow, or the next day, when the snow stops flying, I will take you there. Then all of you are free to leave. I will not harm you."

Red Horn spoke rapidly to the warriors. Four stepped in front of the line of women and former troopers and returned their weapons. As they did, Red Horn explained, "I give them back to prove my honesty and show my good faith. Once more, I will take you up the canyon when the snow stops flying." He stood, nodded, and strode from the tepee.

The two elders went next, then the warriors filed outside, leaving Fargo and the others facing Fast Elk and Lame Hawk. Lame Hawk spoke to Fast Elk, who signed to Fargo, "They go now. I take the white men to a tepee."

Fargo told the others, "All of you are the luckiest people alive. Your decision to tell the truth got you out of a bad situation." He made sure they saw him looking at their guns when he added, "I suggest you don't try anything foolish with those. Sid, you and Everett go with this man. He'll take you to a tepee. You women go back to yours. Melody, we'll head west when the snow lifts."

They left the medicine man sitting alone, staring into the fire. Outside, Fargo heard him chanting, and muttered, "Talking to Shoshoni spirits. Wonder what he's saying."

Fargo repositioned the ventilation flaps and carried another armload of firewood inside his tepee. He rekindled his fire and set the pot to boil more coffee. After he drank a cup, he undressed, stretched out, and drifted asleep.

The soft sound of the tepee door flap being drawn back jarred his eyes open. He cocked his Colt beneath the beaver-pelt pillow and eyed the door. A Levi's-clad leg entered followed by the rest of Melody. Their eyes met. Hers held the unmistakable sheen of lust, his acceptance. Neither spoke. No words were necessary.

He watched her unbuckle and toss her gun belt aside, then loosen her shirt buttons and shuck the garment. She tweaked both nipples erect, then rubbed her breasts, all the time never taking her eyes off his and circling the tip of her tongue around her slightly parted lips.

She moved to stand across the fire from him. Their eyes stayed locked, their stares communicating more than words. Her hands lowered and unbuttoned the Levi's and released the belt buckle. The waistband slipped down till it caught on her hip bones. A fluff of glistening light-red pubic hair appeared. She raised one foot, then the other, to remove her boots. Slowly, she worked the Levi's down to her ankles and stepped out of them.

He watched as she spread her feet and inched closer to the flickering flames. She untied the yellow bow holding her hair in place behind her head, then shook her head to make the hair trail down over her chest. Her head tilted back and she cupped the right breast with one hand and teased her fiery patch with the other.

Aroused, Fargo watched and waited, knowing there would be more before she came to him to fulfill her desires.

Melody turned her back to the fire and looked at him over her shoulder. She patted her rump to draw his attention to it. When he lowered his gaze onto the shapely cheeks and sensuous crack, she bent at the waist and spread them to show her lower charm.

She struck other equally provocative poses to tantalize him before she came to kneel beside him. She pulled the covering robe back to expose his body and started caressing it, first with light touches, then more firmly and rougher, constantly inching her firm breasts toward his lips.

As Fargo took the left nipple between his teeth, her hips rose and she moved his right hand to feel her hot joy. He probed with his middle finger to set her juices flowing and moisten the tight gateway. Only then did she make a sound, a soft murmur. When she did, she pressed the breast into his mouth and lowered her hips, encouraging him to probe deeper. Her breathing quickened and she rolled her hips to make the finger glide up and down the dilating opening.

Finally, she pulled his head back and kissed him openmouthed, gasping hotly, "Take me, Fargo . . . take me, now."

He pulled her down on him. Together they rolled her underneath. She parted her legs and worked his crown between her eager lips. He entered slowly and fully. As he did, she whimpered, "Oh, oh . . . yes, yes . . . give me all of it, please . . . I want it all."

When he withdrew halfway to thrust, she squirmed down to position the top of her slickness to rub against his hard member. He felt her hips rise in preparation for the deep insertion. When he accommodated her, she bit his chest and raked his hard butt with her fingernails. He thrust and gyrated. She shrieked, "Oh, my God! Jesus, Fargo . . . more . . . harder!"

He reached down and cupped her buttock cheeks in his hands and lifted her to meet his pumping. Her legs came up and she locked her ankles around his waist, raising her hot vee into position for maximum pleasure. As he rotated one way, she gyrated in the other, and moaned, "Faster . . . oh, go faster, Fargo . . . deeper too . . . that's it . . . yes, yes. Oh, God, yes, that's it!"

He worked a hand between their sweating bodies and squeezed her breasts. Her back arched and she screamed, "Aaaayeeeiii. Squeeze harder. You won't hurt me. Aaaaagh!"

She writhed beneath him, her lips and teeth sliding from one side of his powerful chest to the other, her heels digging into his buttocks, and her fingernails clawing on his back. He felt her tremble an instant before her tunnel spasmed around his throbbing member. She gasped, "Now, Fargo . . . explode with me. Aaaayeeeiii! Oh, God, yes . . . flood me . . . oh, that's so hot . . . so good."

Her legs opened wide and dropped onto the robe. She whimpered while he continued to give them both additional pleasure. Finally, they lay limp and panting. She hugged him and squirmed close and kissed him. He held her hips and rolled her on top of him. She favored him with hot wet kisses on the shoulders, throat, and ears. He suckled on her nipples and she mewed, "Oh, Jesus, that's good. I'll be sore from top to bottom tomorrow, but I won't mind."

She knelt beside him and started kissing down his torso. Her tongue probed around inside his navel, then moved down and licked his organ. When it stiffened somewhat, her lips encircled the summit and slipped down. She gurgled, "Come on, Fargo . . . help me." She took his left hand and placed it on her breasts and squeezed.

He pulled on the nipples and coaxed her to raise her ass. She did, and he circled her lower charm with two fingers. She cried, "I want you again, Fargo. Please?"

He moved her to straddle him and sit on it. He felt himself slip inside. She leaned back and grasped his knees for balance and leverage, then thrust her moist vee against his hardness and wailed, "That's so good . . . so damn good . . . don't quit, Fargo . . . please, don't stop."

They came together a second time, then she fell forward, breathing hard. He brushed a strand of hair from her face and kissed her. She framed his chiseled face in her hands and swayed her head with a rolling motion to caress his lips and tongue with hers. She got her breath back slowly. Between labored breathings, she gasped, "Fargo, do you like me?"

He'd heard the question before. Most of his women asked "Love me?" not, "Like me?" Perhaps the heretofore haughty widow couldn't bring herself to say, "Love." Regardless, he'd found it a trapping question. He'd also learned that females trapped best when lying on their naked backs. He rolled them onto their sides, cuddled her backside to him, and draped his left arm over her at the chest.

She entwined his fingers in hers and asked, "Well, do you?"

He sidestepped the trap by baiting her with questions of his own. "What do you mean? What are you trying to say?"

She tightened her grip. He took it as a sign she felt encouraged. She expanded her query. "When two people like each other, they're comfortable enough to share their thoughts, their dreams and hopes."

"Go ahead, Melody, tell me your secret."

She turned her head and looked at him over her shoulder. Even in the dim firelight he saw the astonishment in her expression. She whispered, "Secret?"

"Yes. Isn't that what you are leading up to?"

She rolled to face him. Her eyes searched his as she absentmindedly drew tiny circles on his shoulder. After a moment she said, "I admit there are times when you confuse me. Sometimes there is a predictable pattern to your life, your ways, habits, and so forth. Other times there is no telling what you will do. Maybe it is the unpredictable side of you that holds me. Does that make any sense?"

"Some." He wanted to say her paradox itself was predictable. Some people simply had one foot in the mold and the other out of it. They could, depending on the situation, go either way. He was one who could. But, he thought, she wants more than some. He said, "You're wanting to ask me a question or tell me something. Don't fish in my mind, Melody. Spit it out."

"You deserve more than this." Her hand left his shoulder and sliced an arc in the dancing shadows of the flames. "Oh, I know you're comfortable living in a tepee, brewing coffee in a tin pot on an open fire, sleeping day in and day out on the ground. I can understand it. Mature females often hold on to their dolls from childhood. It makes them feel secure."

"Melody, you're rambling. I'm not insecure. Are you?"

"Yes. But that's not so strange. All women search for security. I'm no different."

"I see. Only your ways are different. Is that it, Melody?"

"Not necessarily. You men are naturally secure. You don't have to think about it. Women do. I do. And we have to use everything at our command, do whatever is required, even if it's, er, improper."

"And you lying naked with me was improper?"

She put her back to him and placed his hand on her soft belly. Her long silence conveyed she was deep in thought. Perhaps she was wrestling with her secret, wondering whether or not to reveal it. He felt her take a deep breath. She sighed and began, "I was improper with Selman Davies and Major Cunningham. Fargo, let me take you away from here, this life. Come east with me, to New York, to London, and Paris. We can have everything, do what we want. It's at our fingertips. All we have to do is reach out and take it."

The payroll, he thought, but said, "Davies got to you."

"Yes. But I was ready and willing. As long as Julian was in the army, we were boxed in with only one way to go. I wanted out. Julian wouldn't listen. He didn't care. The army was Julian's security. I hated it. Yes, I was vulnerable and at my wit's end when Selman came along."

"He promised you many things, didn't he, Melody?"

"Of course he did. He said all the things I wanted to hear. He opened a door. I walked through it and didn't look back."

"The door led to Major Cunningham. I presume he—"

"Major Cunningham," she interrupted, "was Colonel Pearson's executive officer at Fort Kearny. Ira Cunningham and I go a long way back. He and I spent time together the summer I turned seventeen. I won't draw you a word picture of our relationship. Anyhow, I arranged with him to assign Julian to lead the payroll detachment."

"So, in the name of security, you sent your husband to his death."

She spun to face him. Her widened eyes were filled with shock. "Oh, no, that wasn't it at all. Before Julian left, I told him about the attack, when and where it would occur. Julian knew. I forewarned him. We had a big argument before he realized what it—the money—would mean for him, for us. In the end he went along with Selman's plan."

"And the three of you were to meet in Seattle?"

"That's right. I didn't know they were dead until tonight, when Red Horn said he killed them. I waited and waited in Cincinnati for word from Julian. I nearly went crazy cooped up in that house, wondering what happened, why I hadn't heard from him. Selman told me the Shoshoni would be in on it. In the end that's all I had to go on. Fargo, I was desperate. Staying in Cincinnati wasn't accomplishing anything. I decided to go to Seattle. As fate would have it, I ran into you." She became excited and poked a finger on his chest to emphasize her next comment. "Don't you see, honey?"

"No," he admitted, "but I have the feeling you're about to help me."

"Fate, Fargo, fate! Fate is a series of events over which we have no control. They happen in one's life and form that person or their destiny. Honey, your fate and mine brought us together and has us in this horrible tepee right now. We're destined to have that payroll and use it for greater things than this. We belong in the high societies of New York and Europe. Can't you see that?"

There's only one hitch, he thought. Fate doesn't have a damn thing to do with it. You're either in the right place at the right time, or the wrong place at the wrong time. In either event luck takes over. He replied, "Well, honey, I'll think about it, but don't get your hopes up. I happen to like it out here in the woods."

She nuzzled his throat, then rolled onto her side and snuggled his organ between her crack. Placing his hand on her bosom, she mumbled, "I will have it."

He knew that she meant the money and that he'd do nothing to help her get it. Once she left the tepee she would be on her own. Fargo went to sleep.

A soft rustling sound jolted his wild-creature hearing. He cocked one eye and watched her dress. When she slipped outside, he closed the eye.

Fargo drifted back to sleep wondering if the cousins and their tongueless uncle were still out there, whether they were solid ice or warm as biscuits fresh from the oven.

13

A commotion outside—running feet, shouts of urgency —awakened Fargo. He looked up through the top opening and saw blue sky. He got up and went to the entrance to see what the ruckus was about. Three Shoshoni women were pointing at something and shouting. Two others ran through zigzag pathways in the snow. He followed the women's point and saw nothing to cause their excitement. He withdrew, remade his fire, and lay back down.

Within minutes the door flap flew open. Fast Elk came inside and squatted by the fire. His expression foretold something bad was happening.

Fargo signed, "What is wrong?"

"The cannon is gone," signed Fast Elk.

Fargo propped on an elbow. "The white women and men?"

Fast Elk's head shook. He signed, "I will see." As he left to go check on them, Fargo started pulling on his clothes.

They met halfway to the women's tepee. Again Fast Elk shook his head. "Gone," he signed.

"The men?" Fargo asked.

Fast Elk motioned Fargo to follow him. They hurried through a labyrinth of paths that led to a tepee on the fringe of the camp. Fast Elk slapped on the covering and shouted his name. There was no response. They exchanged quick glances, then Fargo pulled the flap back. A warrior and two women lay bound, hand and foot, and tied to tepee poles. All three were gagged. Fast Elk released the warrior's gag. After a brief conversation, Fast Elk explained the obvious, "The white men stole away in the night."

Fargo untied one of the women and signed to Fast Elk, "Let's go. Take me to Red Horn."

Coursing through the narrow passageways in the camp proper, they saw Red Horn standing outside his tepee. They went to him, and Fargo said, "The white men and women have left."

Red Horn nodded slowly and grinned. "I know. I listened to them take the cannon. What I do not understand is why they need it."

"They don't," Fargo replied. "I'm as puzzled as you. Let's take a look where it stood, then go to the corral."

Deep ruts left by the cannon's carriage wheels made a beeline for the canyon where Red Horn had said the payroll wagon was located. Fargo counted three sets of shod hoofprints, two pulling the cannon, the other following alongside. He told Red Horn what he suspected. "The women or men didn't take it. The other three men tracking us took it. Look at how fresh their tracks are. I think they watched the others leave, put two and two together, then followed with the cannon. Let's go to the corral and see."

At the corral they followed hoofprints of the five missing horses a short distance into the trees. Fargo analyzed them while Red Horn looked on with keen interest. "This set is old. It was still snowing when they were made." He fingered the depth where it was packed solid, then moved to another set and measured the snow in one. "This rider went before that one I just checked. I'd say by five minutes, no more." He moved to another set and measured. "About the same time as the first set." He checked the other two and found them the freshest. He stood and rubbed his chin, saying, "Three left about the same time."

"The women," Red Horn muttered.

"I believe so. Compared to the fresher prints, they suggest lighter riders. The women went first, but not together. The men came much later, just before it stopped snowing. Everybody struck out to get the money. The three men watched them go before taking the cannon."

Red Horn cocked an eyebrow. "They don't want the money?"

"Oh, yes," Fargo answered. "My guess is they intend to use the cannon to slaughter the others. They will wait until the others have the payroll, or show them where it is, then cut loose on them with everything they have. How far is it to the payroll wagon?"

"Long ride," Red Horn answered. "You go?"

Fargo nodded. "Why not? Show the way, Chief."

Red Horn balked. "No, Trailsman, I don't go. They are fools. They will freeze in the canyon. You go watch." Red Horn turned and strode toward the encampment.

Fargo signed to Fast Elk, "Will you show me the wagon?"

The warrior nodded.

They rode east to a path where the riders went down a long, sloping decline. There Fast Elk halted and signed, "Go wagons." He pointed north, then gave Fargo a choice. "We follow?" Facing due north, he signed the other option, "We go watch?"

Fargo chose the latter. Fast Elk reined hard left and moved back among the trees, where their mounts had better footing. They rode inside the tree line, which traced along the irregular western rim of the canyon. After going more than a mile, Fast Elk angled off and left the trees. Here the rim of the canyon was studded with sheets of slate that countless winds and rains had eroded to resemble castle turrets. They halted and dismounted.

Fast Elk stepped into one of the notches and looked down. Fargo stood beside him. The canyon below was shaped like a long narrow hourglass turned on its side. They stood at the most constricted point. The eastern side of the canyon mirrored the western; barren except for the snaggled-toothed appearance of the slate. At the northern end of the box canyon a rocky wall rose at least two hundred feet before joining the gradual slope of a mountain. Its peak towered far above the tree line. The slope itself was as barren as the canyon, and covered by deep snow.

A great collection of wagons were parked helter-skelter on the canyon floor where the sheer rocky wall began. The Shoshoni had removed the canvas tops from those that had them. Exposed, the beds had quickly filled with snow. Most were Conestogas. Fargo counted six Owensboros and three California flat-beds. He scanned them to spot the payroll wagon. He saw it near the rear at the center.

The five who fled the camp had passed through the narrow part of the hourglass and were nearing the wagons, with Melody the closest. Victoria followed in the stallion's path by about ten lengths. Judith lagged behind her at least twenty lengths. Sid came next, the face of Everett's horse brushing his mount's tail. They were no more than twenty yards behind Judith and closing fast.

Fargo watched Cal and Leon tow the cannon through the narrow slot. Rick's horse plunged through the snow on the far rim, eye level with Fargo. Rick rode well ahead of his relatives, obviously hurrying to get into position so he could spot for them when the time came.

Fast Elk stepped through the notch and squatted to watch and wait. That none of the eight had fired a shot came as no surprise to Fargo. They would get down to the killing when one found the money.

Melody came alongside a Conestoga and dismounted. She fought her way through the snowdrifts to go deeper among the wagons. Fargo saw she was wide of the mark. Victoria halted the Appaloosa next to the stallion, dismounted, and began searching to the far right of Melody. Judith and the two ex-army troopers arrived at the same time. After conversing, they dismounted and split up. Fargo reckoned the trio had made a pact.

Fargo watched Rick give hand signals to Cal and

Leon. Rick waved them forward until they were within point-blank range of the packed wagons. Leon sighted down the barrel while Cal muscled the left wheel to get the cannon aligned. They loaded powder and ball, then Cal waved to Rick that they were ready.

Sid spotted the payroll wagon. Fargo saw him turn and motion to Everett. They looked about to check on the location of the others. Sid moved to get clear shots at Judith and Victoria, Everett to take out Melody. As they got into position and drew their six-guns, Judith apparently sensed something was wrong and dived to safety behind a Conestoga. Sid's bullet thudded into the side of the big wagon.

All hell broke loose, each emptying their weapons at another. Sid ducked and went to the payroll wagon. He rolled over its side and dropped into the snow-filled bed. Everett hurried toward him and took a stance to give him covering fire while he dug around in the snow to find the moneybags.

The cannon roared. The ball tore both sides off an Owensboro, caromed into a California flat-bed, and shattered it. Melody's screams echoed in the thunder from the cannon blast. Rick started firing at Sid and Everett. Cal reloaded the cannon.

Fast Elk stood and looked north. Again the cannon belched flame and roared. Fast Elk motioned for Fargo to follow his gaze. Fargo looked toward the towering mountain and lifted his gaze slowly. He saw it happening near the summit; a jagged horizontal line appeared in the snow all across the mountainside.

He watched the fault line widen and the snow below it lurch. The avalanche was in movement, and nothing could stop it. Those fighting below were unaware, not that it mattered, for no one could possibly escape.

Tons of snow roared down the mountainside, collected tons more, grew in size and strength, raced downward, and exploded over the top of the wall. From the boxed end to the narrow, the canyon was filled with the onrushing avalanche. A mighty cloud of white mushroomed out of the canyon, leaving Fargo and the warrior dusted with powdery snow. The awesome sound rumbled south. An eerie silence settled in its wake.

Fast Elk exhaled and signed, "Shoshoni spirits have spoken."

Fargo wanted to add, "With a little help from U.S. Army ordnance." Instead, he brushed snow off his face and shoulders as he looked for Rick. He saw him mounting up at the edge of the tree line and shouted, "You're mine, Rick. There's no place to hide."

Rick fired two wild shots toward him before reining south.

Fargo signed to Fast Elk, "I am going after him."

The warrior nodded, but made no move to mount up and go with him.

Fargo urged the Ovaro south along the rim at a murderous pace, staying in the earlier path as much as possible. At the first opportunity he went down the rocky slope and into the lower end of the canyon. On the far side he easily picked up Rick's trail and rode in it to a thicket surrounded on three sides by an outcrop of large rocks. Rick had dismounted and led his horse behind the dense growth.

Fargo skirted the outcrop. He had reached the halfway point around it when Rick fired. The slug whizzed past Fargo's head and buried in the trunk of a pine. The Trailsman slid to the ground and scrambled for cover behind a fallen Douglas fir. "It's no use, Rick," he yelled. "Even if you get me—and you won't— there's no place to go. Red Horn's warriors will have your scalp by sundown."

He watched the outcrop for movement. Sooner or later Rick would get restless and commit an error. An hour passed, then another. The sun lowered beyond the rugged mountains. Evening shadows crept over the area. Fargo waited to make his move until the faint light of day all but disappeared. He threw a dead branch toward the outcrop. Rick's gun barked twice, one of the bullets crunching into the branch. Between the shots, Fargo sprang left and raced for the thicket.

Rick fired into the thicket blindly three times. Fargo twisted a limb from a scrub oak, put his hat on one end of the stick, and held it up for Rick to see the crown. A bullet broke the limb below the hat.

Fargo dashed around the thicket into the outcrop and caught Rick reloading. Fargo dived onto him and wrenched the gun from Rick's hand. He powered two fists into Rick's face. The youngster collapsed. Fargo threw the empty Joslyn away, then searched Rick for a hideout or a knife. Satisfied the youngster was completely unarmed, he picked him up and draped him over his saddle.

They were crossing the floor of the canyon when Rick came to. Fargo said, "Kid, I wouldn't be in your place for anything in this world."

"Lemme go," Rick groaned. "Why didn't you kill me and get it over with?"

"Let's say I don't like shooting children. I'm giving you to the Shoshoni. They'll make a man out of you, or kill you in the trying."

"Naw, mister, you didn't kill me 'cause you need me, so don't give me that Shoshoni bullshit."

Fargo halted and looked at him. "Oh, what do you mean by that? Why in blazes would I need the likes of you?"

"Mister, I ain't as dumb as you think. You need me to help dig out that payroll."

Fargo nudged the pinto forward. He repeated Red Horn's earlier question concerning the payroll, "What money?"

"I said I wasn't stupid. You know what money."

"I didn't see any. Did you?"

"No, not actually, but it's there, and you know it, same as me, same as everybody else."

"What makes you think they were looking for money? I don't recall seeing or hearing you talk to any of them about money."

"Act dumb if you want to, mister, but you know as well as me that that woman hired you to bring her here to fetch the payroll her old man stole. She tried to pull a fast one on you, didn't she? Women are like that."

Fargo didn't answer until they were back in camp and walking to Red Horn's tepee. "There's only one flaw in your thinking, Rick. I suppose I should say, one thaw. I wouldn't need you or anybody else to help me get that payroll. All I'd need to do is wait for the spring thaw to show it to me."

Red Horn stepped out of the tepee just as they arrived. He looked at Rick. "Fast Elk told me you went after one, Trailsman. He stole my cannon?"

"Sure did. Where do you want him?"

"We go sit in Spirit Tepee. Bring him."

On the way Red Horn called out to Lame Hawk inside the spirit tepee, then sent a warrior to get Fast Elk.

Fargo and Rick waited outside while the medicine man purified the interior.

Fast Elk, bundled in a bighorn sheepskin, joined them. He signed to Fargo, "I made a fire in your tepee."

Fargo thanked him. The door flap swung open. Smoke boiled out. The medicine man waved them inside. Fargo shoved Rick down to sit next to Fast Elk, facing Red Horn and Lame Hawk, who sat on the other side of the fire.

Red Horn's studious gaze made Rick nervous. Rick whined, "Why's he staring at me like that? I ain't done nothing to him."

Red Horn spoke to Fast Elk. The warrior rose, stepped in front of Rick, and drew his knife. Rick gulped. Fargo told him, "Sonny boy, one more peep out of you and you can kiss your scalp good-bye." He signed to Fast Elk, "Let him feel the knife."

Fast Elk slashed. A thin ribbon of blood appeared on Rick's left cheek. The warrior stared hard at him for a long moment, then went back and sat in his place.

Red Horn looked at Rick and said, "When the sun comes, you will bring my cannon back."

Fargo said, "Chief Red Horn, with your permission, I will return in the spring season to find the money."

Red Horn grunted, "You want the army money?"

"No. I will take it to the army."

"Trailsman, there is no money. The white men's scalps on my staff were not taken from Davies and the army officer. They have the army money."

Fargo suppressed the urge to chuckle. He asked, "Do you know where they went?"

"To the great waters, to—" He paused to talk with Lame Hawk, then said, "San Frisco. You go there, Trailsman?"

Fargo had no intention of changing his plans. He would report it to the army. They could do what they wanted. He looked at Red Horn and shook his head.

Rick stuttered, "Y-y-you mean I, went through all th-that for nothing?"

Fargo answered, "Look at it this way, Rick. You got to see one hell of an avalanche."

Red Horn added, "Shoshoni spirits say you stay here long time. You help old women do work. Cut lots of wood. Clean my cannon. I give you to Chases Horses." The chief stood, spoke to Fast Elk, then left.

In broken English Lame Hawk muttered, "Shoshoni spirits say go now."

Outside, Fast Elk hurried to a tepee and returned with an old, obese woman. He signed to Fargo that her name was Chases Horses. The woman walked around Rick, eyed him up and down, pinched both his arms, and pried his mouth open to look at his teeth. Satisfied he was sound, she felt his privates, made a face, and grunted. Fast Elk interpreted her grunt. "Chases Horses not happy."

"What'd they say?" Rick wanted to know.

"She said she's going to cut your balls off," Fargo replied. "He said not until you retrieve the cannon. If I were you, Rick, I'd work damn slow and honey up to her every chance I got. You'll have it licked once you get past the smell. It's that or start talking in high soprano."

Rick stared at the woman and balled his fists.

Chases Horses smirked as she drove her right fist into his gut. Rick doubled over, gasping. She curled an arm around his waist and carried him away. Fast Elk shrugged. Fargo went to his tepee.

The two young maidens, Blue Sage and Laughing Bear, glanced up and smiled when he entered. Both were naked and waiting.

Fargo released his gun belt, thinking he might change his plans after all and winter here with the hospitable Shoshoni.

He took the thought as a clear sign the Shoshoni spirits intended for him to remain.

He heard Rick scream, "Lemme go, old woman. Give my pants back."

Chuckling, Fargo pulled off his boots.

LOOKING FORWARD!
The following is the opening
section from the next novel in the exciting
Trailsman series from Signet:

**THE TRAILSMAN #102
THE CORONADO KILLERS**

*1860, the southwest corner of the
Arizona Territory,
where it borders Mexico and the lower end
of California, an almost forgotten land
waiting for those with ambition and greed . . .*

Danger was all around him.

He could feel it, hear it, smell it, almost taste it. Everything but see it in the inky blackness of the night and the driving, howling downpour. Arizona. The land the Indians called the place of little springs, the dry land. But when the rains came it was anything but dry. Rivulets became screaming cascades of water. Streams grew into racing torrents of brown, churning fury. The normally dry, harmless arroyos that made up much of the land flooded and became driving maelstroms that swept everything along in their path.

The very ground grew soft, turned into sucking mud and crumbling edges that could sweep horse and rider into one of the racing channels of water. The skies had burst open almost three hours ago as the big man with the lake-blue eyes rode westward through the night. By day, he'd have had a chance to see the dark purple clouds gather and roll across the land, but by night he could only feel the change in atmospheric pressure that signaled the storm. This one had moved in with furious speed, and he'd barely had time to don his rain slicker.

He could do nothing but continue to ride across the flat land. I'm lost, Skye Fargo told himself as he moved the Ovaro at an aimless walk through a world made of driving rain, unable to see even a few feet ahead. Mostly he feared the racing rivers of water he could hear all around him. One misstep, a wrong turn, and he and the Ovaro could be plunged into one of the raging torrents. Fargo's lips pulled back in a grimace as he rode with his head down against the driving rain. He strained to hear any change in the sound of the rushing waters that would warn him he was too close or a torrent had shifted its course. Then suddenly there was a sound, different, cutting through the hissing roar of the water. He inclined his head to one side. It cut through again, a woman's voice crying out. He lifted his head and wiped the rain from his face. No, not a cry, he corrected himself, a call. The woman was calling for someone and he suddenly saw the faint glow through the downpour.

The glow moved as he watched. A lantern. He heard the woman call again. Fargo edged the Ovaro forward ever so slowly and listened to the hiss of rushing water on his left. He moved toward the light and watched it grow brighter, slanting lines of rain growing visible as he neared. "Jeff," the woman's voice called out again, words distinguishable now. "Jeff, Jeff . . ." she called and Fargo heard the panic in her voice. He halted the Ovaro and swung to the ground.

"Over here," he called out and saw the lantern turn toward him. The woman's figure took shape behind it, all but hidden in a full-length poncho with a hood.

"Who are you calling in this damned rainstorm? It's dangerous out here," Fargo said.

"My little boy," the woman said. "He sleepwalks. He got out and wandered off. Oh, God, I hope I'm not too late. I didn't realize he was gone until at least fifteen minutes afterward."

Fargo peered under the hood of the poncho and managed to glimpse a pair of eyes in a wide face. "Why'd you walk this way? Or maybe you're just wandering," he said.

"No. When he sleepwalks he goes straight south from the house," the woman said. "Of course, it's all dry land usually. I started south. I don't know if I'm lost or not."

"I don't know, either," Fargo said as he strained to see into the rain and blackness. To find the boy would be like looking for the proverbial needle in a haystack, only this haystack was made of a sudden watery death. "Give me the lantern," he said, and the woman handed him the light. He raised it over his head, reached as high as he could with it, and the circle of light pushed out a few feet farther. Far enough to let him glimpse the edge of a leaping, rushing cascade of water not more than six feet away. If the boy had fallen into it he'd been swept miles away to his death by now. Fargo turned to the woman and handed the lantern to her. "Keep holding it high," he said as he dropped the Ovaro's reins to the ground so the horse would stay. He took his lariat from the fork swell of the saddle and took the lantern back again from the woman.

Holding the light high in the air, Fargo began to carefully move forward and heard another hissing torrent to his left. He let the sounds on both sides keep him in the center of the ground as he moved through the darkness, the woman at his heels. "How come the rain didn't snap him awake right away?" Fargo asked.

"He doesn't snap awake. Sleepwalkers take a little while to come around after they wake. He was probably too far from the house by then," the woman said.

Fargo stepped on ground that sucked as it slid from under his feet, and the circle of light showed him the racing torrent to his right was growing larger. Again he felt the ground slide underfoot and cursed silently. It could give way and send him and the woman plunging into the raging floodwaters. He halted and lowered the lamp.

"Can you find your way back to the house?" he asked.

"I think so, but I can't go back. I have to keep looking for Jeff," she said from under the edge of the hood.

"You'll only get yourself killed out here," Fargo said. "You've got to go back. If the boy has found a spot to stay, he'll be there when the rain stops. If he hasn't, you're too late now." He pulled his lips back in distaste at the harshness of his words, true as they were. He reached out and she took the lantern.

"I can't," she said. "I have to keep looking."

"Go back," he said, gentleness in his voice this time. "It's the only thing you can do now."

She made no reply and the hooded poncho suddenly seemed empty and filled with blackness. He was about to urge her again to retrace steps when a sound caught his ears. Faint, more of a whimper than a cry, he halted, strained to listen, and heard the sound again. "Wait," he said and took the lantern from the woman. "How old is Jeff?" he asked.

"Six," the woman said, and Fargo began to move forward again with the light held in front of him. He felt the woman's steps rush after him.

"Slow, dammit," he said harshly, and she pulled back at once. The faint, whimpering sound came again, directly ahead, and Fargo raised the lantern higher and peered forward as he edged his way through the driving rain. The dim circle of light probed ahead of him, and suddenly he saw the small, huddled shape, looking more like a dark mound than a child. And just behind the shape, Fargo saw the two cascading streams of water come together in a V to form a deeper, wider torrent of raging floodwater. He saw the woman's form brush by him as she glimpsed the small mound and her half sob of relief rose into the night. "No, easy," Fargo called out, but she was at the boy already and dropping to one knee.

"Oh, Jeff, my baby, oh, you're all right. Thank God, thank God," the woman sobbed in relief as she hugged the boy to her. She rose with him, a quick, sharp movement that dug her feet into the ground. Fargo cursed as he saw her suddenly go down, her feet sliding out from under her. "Run, Jeff, run," she had the presence of mind to scream, and the boy ran forward as his mother disappeared into the racing, churning torrent. Fargo caught the boy with one arm, his other hand holding the lantern.

"Stay here," he ordered the boy as he rushed forward and heard the woman's screams. He raised the lantern to see her clinging to the branch of a gnarled mesquite tree that had somehow remained rooted deep enough in the soil to withstand the waters that pulled at it. Fargo moved as close as he dared to the edge of the soil that had crumbled to plunge the woman into the water, set the lantern down, and began to twirl the lariat over his head. He measured distance, calculated the weight of the rain that would bear upon the lariat as it sailed through the air. The woman could only cling a few moments longer, he knew, her body pulled almost horizontal by the clutching waters. He'd have to throw the rope over her. She'd have only a split second to let go of the branch and grab hold of the lariat. He cursed as he let the rope fly through the rainswept air.

He'd calculated well, he realized, as he saw the lariat land over her head, fall onto her shoulders. He watched with a grimace as the woman let go of the tree branch. The raging waters tore her away at once, but Fargo saw that she had managed to grab hold of the lariat and pull it under her arms. He tightened the loop at once and felt the shock in his shoulder muscles as her weight and the pull of the water struck at the loop of rope. He began to pull, braced in the muddy soil with his heels dug deeply, and felt the floodwaters fight back, unwilling to give up their prize. But using all the power in his massive shoulders and powerful arms, he began to pull the woman toward him. He halted for a moment as his arm muscles began to cramp, then continued pulling until he saw the hooded poncho reach the edge of the soil that had given way. He pulled again and saw her arms come up, hands dig into the rain-soaked soil to help pull herself forward.

He continued to pull and pushed his way backward with his heels as the woman came up onto firmer ground, free of the raging waters. But he let the lariat go slack only when he saw her rise to her feet and come toward him. She dropped to her knees beside him, her voice a hoarse gasp from inside the hood. "Thank you. Oh, God, thank you," she murmured, and he pressed one hand on her shoulder. He let her catch her breath a few minutes longer, grateful for the time to let the pain subside in his own shoulder muscles. When he pushed to his feet, she came up with him and hurried the few yards to where the little boy sat with his knees drawn up under his chin. Fargo stepped past her to where the Ovaro had waited without moving so much as a foreleg. The woman hurried after him, and he took the boy from her and lifted him into the saddle. He stayed beside the horse with his right arm around the small form as the woman took the lantern and led the way. He used his keen hearing to mark the rushing waters that roared and hissed all around them.

"No, to the right," he said at one point and then, at another, "You're getting too close. Stay left." The woman followed his words, and they seemed to wander for hours though he knew it was only minutes. He kept his arm around the little boy in the saddle when suddenly the rain lessened and a soft glow of distant light cut through the darkness.

"There . . . the house," the woman said and started

to turn toward it too abruptly. Fargo reached forward and caught her arm and she stopped.

"The water's too close. No sharp turns," he said. "Make a wide circle." The hood nodded and he slowly followed the caped figure in a wide turn. Finally the light grew brighter and the dark outlines of the house appeared behind it. When they reached the open doorway and the shaft of yellow light that streamed into the night, he swung little Jeff from the saddle and the woman hurried the boy into the house.

"The stable's in back. I'll have coffee ready," she said, and Fargo nodded and led the Ovaro around the house, which turned out to be larger than it first appeared to be. He found a spacious, dry stable with two horses inside and a lantern affording enough light for him to unsaddle the Ovaro, take a rubbing cloth from a wall peg, and give the horse a fast drying. He put the horse into a wide stall when he finished, saw to a full pail of oats, and returned to the house. The rain had begun to come down hard again when he stepped into a well-furnished room, a deep settee to one side and a lounging chair nearby. A fireplace cast a soft glow on a braided rug on the floor as the woman stepped into the room. She had a blue robe wrapped around her, and he saw brown hair and light brown eyes, a strong face with wide cheekbones and a wide mouth. He guessed her at somewhere between thirty-five and forty, a few lines around the wide mouth but a face with real attractiveness still in it. "Take those muddy clothes off and I'll give you a sheet to wrap around yourself," she said. He pulled the rain slicker off, and she paused to gaze at him for a moment before hurrying into another room.

When she returned with the sheet, he was down to underdrawers, and he saw her take in the powerful symmetry of his muscular torso before handing him the sheet. "Jeff's asleep. He'll stay that way. He's exhausted," she said and closed the door. "Thanks to you, mister, he's not dead. Nor am I."

"Fargo . . . Skye Fargo." He smiled and finished tying the sheet around his lower torso.

"Carrie Thompson, Fargo," she said and let a wide smile light her attractive face. "I can't say anything but thank you, and that seems shamefully poor."

"It'll do fine," he said.

"Be right back," Carrie Thompson said and hurried into the kitchen to return with two mugs of steaming coffee. "I put some whiskey in it. Figured we could both use it."

"You figured right," Fargo said as he took one of the mugs, sipped, and let the delicious taste roll in his mouth and warm his body as he swallowed. "You're here alone. Your husband off someplace?" he asked.

"He died just before Jeff was born. More than six years now. He took the fever and just went," Carrie Thompson said and instant sadness touched her face for a moment.

"Sorry," Fargo said. "And an attractive woman such as you hasn't found a man since?"

"The pickings are slim around here, Skye Fargo. My husband was a good man. I won't settle for just a pair of trousers. I've managed to raise Jeff on my own. Maybe things will be different when we move."

"You planning that?"

"Some time. I've a hundred head of longhorns and a steady buyer in Tucson. That's fine for now, but there's not much here for a growing boy. I'll want to be moving on with Jeff one day," Carrie said.

"You handle a hundred head all by yourself?"

"I've an old cowpuncher who comes in three times a week to help. Together we get things done," Carrie said as he drained the mug. She rose to take the empty mug from him, and the robe fell open enough for him to see a strong but shapely calf with the kind of firm skin a much younger woman would be proud to have. "It's lonely, but things will get better in time," Carrie said, and Fargo smiled and gazed into space. "What are you thinking, Fargo?" Carrie inquired.

"That you're a proud, strong woman with a good way of looking at things," he said.

"That's nice to hear," she said, put her head back, and finished the last of the coffee in the mug. The robe swung wide again and he saw a flash of thigh as firm and youthful as the calf. "I've an extra room. You'll stay the night, I hope," she said. "The rain's still coming down hard."

"I'd appreciate that," Fargo nodded, and she stepped to him, her wide mouth serious, brown eyes searching his face.

"I meant what I said about there's no paying for what you did tonight. I'm grateful. I'll never stop being that."

"Glad I was there."

"You're no ordinary cowpoke riding a lonely trail," Carrie said. "What were you doing out on such a night?"

"Got caught in the storm and found myself lost. I'm on my way to Mescatel."

"You'll reach it tomorrow. It's not far from here. I do all my town shopping there."

"Sheriff Snyder's expecting me," Fargo said.

"I know Fred Snyder. You a law man?" Carrie asked.

"Not really, though I've done some law work," Fargo told her. "Maybe I'll have more to tell after I meet with the sheriff. I don't know that much yet."

"I'll wash the mud from your things and hang them by the fire to dry. Meanwhile, I'll show you to the room," she said, and he followed her as she lighted another lantern and led him to a small, neat room with a dresser and washbasin and single cot. "Sleep well, Fargo. You deserve it," she said and hurried away. He lay down on the cot, shed the sheet, and felt tiredness flood over him. He closed his eyes and slept at once, waking only when the morning sun streamed through a lone window.

He rose to find his clothes, neat and dry, hung over

the back of a straight chair near the door. He dressed and smelled the coffee before he reached the kitchen. Carrie Thompson turned to him with a bright smile, and he saw she wore a white shirt filled well by deep breasts and a brown skirt over full, wide hips, a woman's figure but with vitality and youthful strength very much part of it. He took the mug of coffee she gave him and went to the open doorway to look out at the land. "Most of the floodwater is gone," he said.

"It's always like that here. The land draws in the water like a sponge once the rain stops. Things dry out fast," Carrie said and came over to where he stood. "Come back for supper when you've finished with Fred Snyder," she said. "I'll have a good meal ready."

"I'd enjoy a home-cooked meal," Fargo said.

"Then I'll be expecting you," she said and put her arm in his as she walked to the stable with him. A small explosion of energy ran around a corner of a large barn and headed for them, and he saw the boy properly for the first time. He had his mother's wide cheekbones in his unlined child's face along with her brown eyes.

" 'Morning, Jeff," Fargo said. "How are you feeling this morning?"

"Very good, sir," the boy said. "I was real scared last night."

"So was I," Fargo said.

"Ma says you found me and saved our lives," Jeff said, his eyes round as small saucers.

"I was at the right place at the right time. You just get out of that sleepwalking."

"I will," Jeff said and ran off to where an old cowpuncher waited inside a large corral. Fargo saw the longhorns roaming the fenced area. He went into the stable, and Carrie leaned against the wall and watched him saddle up.

"That's a fine-looking horse, Fargo. No ordinary horse and no ordinary rider, I'm thinking. I'm curious why you're on your way to see Sheriff Snyder."

"I'll tell you at supper," he laughed as he swung into the saddle, and she nodded and waved as he rode away at a slow trot. He headed west at once and saw that the ground was amazingly firm though not yet back to its hard, dusty dryness. He scanned the rock formations of sandstone buttresses, pinnacles, and pillars, window rocks and wind-sculptured basalt towers. He passed stepping-stone formations of rock with surprisingly heavy tree cover of Arizona sycamore, canyon live oak and Western spruce. The Apache knew those jagged rock formations and thick tree covers, he thought grimly. This was their land, the White Mountain Apache to the north, the Mescalero Apache to the east, and here the Chirachua Apache. The Pueblo and the Papago had once been strong in Arizona, but now only the Apache remained, undefeated and unbowed.

He rode at a steady pace, stayed due west, and finally saw the buildings of Mescatel rise up out of the heat haze. He rode into a town larger than he'd expected with an inn and a general store. He pulled up as he saw the narrow wood frame building with the words "SHERIFF'S OFFICE" hanging on a sign outside. A man with a silver star lounging in the doorway straightened up as Fargo rode to a halt.

"Fargo, it has to be," the man boomed out. "I was told about that Ovaro of yours. No exaggeration," he added as he took in the magnificent black fore and hind quarters and glistening white midsection of the horse.

"Sheriff Snyder?" Fargo said as he swung to the ground and took the strong hand offered him.

"Yes, sir," the sheriff said. "Ted Greener told me all about you and that Ovaro of yours. Come inside where we can talk." Fargo followed the man into a neat office with three cells in an adjoining back room. He took in a man of some forty-five years, maybe edging fifty, with salt-and-pepper hair and a strong face with a prominent nose and dark blue eyes that held both forthrightness and caution at once. Fargo sank into a chair near the window as Sheriff Snyder perched himself atop his desk.

"That was a powerful lot of money you sent," Fargo said.

"It's a powerful lot I'll be asking," the sheriff answered. "But from what I've heard, you're the one man that can do the job." He was about to go on when the pounding of hooves at a gallop echoed into the office. They came to an abrupt stop just outside the door, and Fargo looked through the window to see a girl leap from a deep-chested bay mare. He glimpsed a dark red shirt and Levis and hair that was tawny rather than blond, the color of wheat when it's in the shade. The sheriff came to peer through the window beside him as the young woman strode toward the door.

"What's all that about?" Fargo asked.

The sheriff spat the word out. "Trouble."